Every line in Gio's face stood out in stark relief. "I told you last night, Valentina, I give you full permission to despise me. And believe me, I have every intention of making you despise me over and over again."

He reached out with two hands and pulled her into him before she could take a breath and then his mouth was fusing to hers. The kiss was desperate and brutal but electrifying. Anger and pain and remorse all clawed up within Valentina, seeking release. Desperately she clutched at his head, holding him to her, allowing no escape. Gio stopped, breathing harshly, his forehead resting on Valentina's. She was dizzy with the sudden overwhelming surge of need mixed with adrenaline.

Hate *me* Valentina…not yourself. This thing…it's out of our control."

SICILY'S CORRETTI DYNASTY

The more powerful the family…the darker the secrets!

Harlequin Presents® introduces the Correttis;
Sicily's most scandalous family!

The Empire

Young, rich and notoriously handsome, the Correttis' legendary
exploits regularly feature in Sicily's tabloid pages!

The Scandal

But how long can their reputations withstand the glaring heat of the
spotlight before their family's secrets are exposed?

The Legacy

Once nearly destroyed by the secrets cloaking their thirst for power,
the new generation of Correttis are riding high again—and no
disgrace or scandal will stand in their way…

Sicily's Corretti Dynasty

Eight volumes to collect—you won't want to miss out!

Abby Green

A SHADOW OF GUILT

SICILY'S
CORRETTI
DYNASTY

HHARLEQUIN PRESENTS®
™

Recycling programs
for this product may
not exist in your area.

ISBN-13: 978-0-373-13160-0

A SHADOW OF GUILT

Copyright © 2013 by Harlequin Books S.A.

Special thanks and acknowledgment are given to Abby Green for her contribution to Sicily's Corretti Dynasty series

Printed in U.S.A.

All about the author...
Abby Green

ABBY GREEN deferred doing a social anthropology degree to work freelance as an assistant director in the film and TV industry—which is a social study in itself! Since then it's been early starts, long hours, mucky fields, ugly car parks and wet weather gear—especially working in Ireland. She has no bona fide qualifications but could probably help negotiate a peace agreement between two warring countries after years of dealing with recalcitrant actors. Since discovering a guide to writing romance one day, she decided to capitalize on her longtime love for Harlequin® romances and attempt to follow in the footsteps of such authors as Kate Walker and Penny Jordan. She's enjoying the excuse to be paid to sit inside, away from the elements. She lives in Dublin and hopes that you will enjoy her stories. You can email her at abbygreen3@yahoo.co.uk.

Other titles by Abby Green available in ebook:

Harlequin Presents®

This is for my fellow Corretti Continuity Comrades. Thanks for the cyber help and support. It was lovely exploring and inhabiting the Corretti world with you all x

CHAPTER ONE

HE SHOULD BE in that coffin, and not his irrepressible best friend.

Giacomo Corretti stood in the shadow of the tall pine tree and watched as the coffin was lowered into the ground just a few feet away from where he was effectively hidden. The tight ball of ice firmly lodged in his gut was slowly spreading out to every extremity. He welcomed this even as he castigated himself for being a coward.

The small group of people around the coffin started to move, the priest's final words of blessing lingering on the warm spring air along with the pungent scent of incense. It shouldn't be warm, Gio suddenly realised, it shouldn't be spring. The sea shouldn't be twinkling benignly under a cerulean sky. He desperately wanted apocalyptic clouds to roll in off stormy waters, for everything to darken and for thunder and lightning to lash this place. To lash *him* to pieces.

He could hear the heartbreaking sound of Mario's mother sobbing as she leant on her aged husband. The sound cut him in two. Gio would never have merited this outpouring of grief. The realisation was stark but brought with it no sense of self-pity.

In contrast, beside them with a stoically straight back stood their tall and narrow-shouldered daughter, Valentina. Her long chestnut hair was tied back in a plait and on her head was a black scarf. The ill-fitting black jacket and skirt she wore hinted at the coltish seventeen-year-old body underneath.

She didn't have to look around for Gio to know every line on her face with instant recall. Pale olive skin as soft as a rose petal. The lush curve of her mouth and lips which more than hinted at a burgeoning womanly sensuality. She had the most extraordinarily coloured eyes, golden brown like amber.

Tiger's eyes.

He could picture them flashing now with mock anger and a little bit of very real anger and fear whenever she'd caught her beloved older brother and Gio flirting with the danger they had loved so much.

As if the intensity of his gaze and thoughts had touched her, Valentina Ferranti turned around and pinpointed the exact spot where Gio stood, those almond-shaped eyes narrowing on him.

It was too late, he couldn't run. She turned fully and looked at him for a long moment. She was pale and her beautiful face was puffy from crying. Her eyes were shadowed and grief-stricken in a way that no one should ever have to deal with before their time. He had done that to her. He had caused this irreparable damage.

His careless words came back to him from that night: *'Don't worry, I'll have him back to his books before midnight just like Cinderella....'*

Valentina's desolation reached out to touch Gio and mock him. And then she was stalking towards him with long slim legs; her hands were curled to fists much like his, by her sides. Her face was contorted with the mad anger of grief.

She stopped just inches away. So close that he could

smell her sweet fresh scent. It was incongruous in the midst of such misery.

'You are not welcome here, Corretti.' Her voice was rough and husky from crying and Gio's insides contracted so much he wondered how he stayed conscious when he couldn't breathe. But he was breathing and he marvelled at the human body's instinct to survive, no matter what.

He took a breath. 'I…' He stopped when the familiar tightening of his vocal chords warned of humiliation to come but he ignored it. 'I…know.'

The fact that he hadn't stumbled over those completely ineffectual words came as small comfort. Mario, her brother and his friend, had been the one who had patiently helped Gio to overcome his chronic stutter which had lasted well into his early teens.

At twenty-two now, the sting of years of humiliation was still like a scar branding his skin. And yet in this moment, he longed to feel that humiliation again. So that he could be subjected to Valentina's cruel laugh and ridicule. Except…she wouldn't do that, she had never done that. She'd always been sweet and shy, and when he had stuttered in front of her she'd never used it as a tool to hurt, as almost everyone else had. Especially his family.

Suddenly Valentina lashed out, taking him by surprise. Her small fist connected with Gio's chest with enough force to send him staggering backwards. Her voice throbbed with pain, 'He was everything to us and thanks to you he's gone. He was going to graduate from university next year and be a success, and you…?'

Valentina's voice was sneering now. 'What can you do for us now? *Nothing.* Get out of here, Corretti. You taint this place with your presence.'

Brokenly she added, 'If you hadn't encouraged him to go out that night—' She stopped and bit her lip fiercely.

The blood drained from Gio's face completely. 'I'm sorry...so sorry,' he said faintly.

Valentina gathered herself once more, eyes dead. 'It's your fault. I hate you, Corretti—I'll hate you for ever because you're alive and he's not.'

Her words fell like splinters of glass all over Gio's skin. She was looking at him now as if she would push him all the way off the nearby cliff and happily watch him crash to pieces on the rocks below.

'Come, Valentina, it's time to go.'

They were both startled from the dark taut energy surrounding them when Valentina's father materialised to take her arm. His voice was thin and weary. 'This is not the time or place.'

Valentina seemed to crumple visibly and without looking at Gio again she allowed her father to turn her and lead her away. After a couple of metres though Mario's father stopped. He looked back to Gio with impossibly mournful eyes and just shook his head sadly. The man had aged ten years in the space of just a few days. It was worse than if he'd spat at Gio's feet or even punched him as Valentina had.

The truth was stark—if Gio hadn't had the unlikeliest of friendships with Mario in the first place, if he hadn't cajoled and pleaded with him to come out that night, this never would have happened.

In that moment Gio wanted to die more than anything else in the world. So badly he could taste it. Everything and anyone he'd ever loved was gone now. For ever. Everything good and promising and hopeful was broken and destroyed.

But, he knew with a bitter taste in his mouth that suicide would be too easy. Far easier than living with this pain every day. Living with the pain of knowing he had decimated an entire family and reduced them to this aching loss. This was his inheritance and he would live with it for the rest of his life.

Seven years later...

It was the wedding of the decade. Two of the most powerful families in Sicily uniting in holy matrimony. Valentina's mouth thinned into a cynical line. Except everyone knew it wasn't a love match between Alessandro Corretti and Alessia Battaglia. It was a bid for the ultimate power play, a way for the Corretti family to go on undefeated into the future for generations to come. If merging with their one-time bitter rivals was what it took, then so be it.

Valentina stopped what she was doing for a moment and put a hand to her chest. Even just thinking of the name Corretti made her feel slightly bilious. Not to mention the fact that she was at this very moment working at their behest.

Much as she would have loved to have been able to tell Carmela Corretti—the mother of the groom—where she could shove her job offer, Valentina didn't have that luxury. She was the owner of a tiny struggling catering company and she'd sweated blood and tears to start it up and try to keep it afloat with her minimal staff. It was the only thing supporting her aged and ailing parents.

Carmela had a reputation, despite the vast Corretti wealth, of being very tight with money, and Valentina knew that part of the reason she'd been lucky enough to get the job had been due to her *very* reasonable prices. Read: ridiculously cheap. But it was the kudos of being hired for something as exclusive as this that would count in the long run, *and* the payment, in spite of not charging as much as her competitors.

As Valentina put the finishing touches to some beluga

caviar canapés she couldn't help recalling Carmela's overly made-up and expressionless face when she'd looked down her patrician nose at Valentina a few weeks previously. 'This has to be the most sophisticated event of the decade—the budget for the food itself will of course be limitless. If you mess this up, Ms Ferranti, you do know you won't ever work on this island again, don't you?'

Valentina had struggled not to look as panic-stricken as she'd felt. The very prospect of having to go to the mainland and leave her parents behind was not an option. Carmela was right though; if Valentina failed at this she would be lucky to get work as a part-time waitress in a pizza joint in Naples.

So she'd stifled the panic and said meekly, 'Of course, Mrs Corretti, I know how important this is.'

And now she and her staff were being paid a pittance to create the most expensive caviar hors d'oeuvres in the world. Carmela had presided over a tasting of the sample menu Valentina had devised and that hour had been the most nerve-racking of Valentina's career so far. And then she'd approved the menu with a mere dismissive flick of her impeccably manicured hand. Valentina had stood there in shock for a long moment before the older woman had spat out, 'Well? What are you waiting for? You have work to do.'

On being given the go-ahead, regal salmon caviar had been flown all the way from Scotland, along with smoked salmon. The beef for the main luncheon had come from Ireland. The beluga caviar had naturally come straight from Russia. The champagne reserved for the head table alone was from the year 1907, salvaged from an infamous shipwreck, its price too astronomical for Valentina to get her head around. The rest of the champagne was merely Bollinger.

No, money was no object when making sure people *saw* and *tasted* the Corretti wealth, they just didn't mind scrimping on the labour behind it.

Valentina blew an errant hair out of her hot face and stood back. Her own two personal staff came by her side and Franco said in awestruck tones at the array of trays of hors d'oeuvres, 'They're like works of art. Val, you've outdone yourself this time.'

Valentina smiled ruefully. 'As much as we need to create the effect, we want them to be eaten.'

She had to admit then that the regal salmon caviar with its distinctive orange colour, wrapped in smoked salmon and in a toasted bread cup, did look enticing. Her stomach rumbled and she looked up at the clock and let out a squeak, tearing off her apron as she did. She fired off commands as she looked for her suit bag which contained her uniform for the day. 'Franco, make sure the chefs are on schedule for the main meal, and, Sara, make sure the serving staff are dressed and ready to take these trays up. We should take the rest of the canapés out of the fridges now. And get Tomasso to check that all the champagne bottles are in the ice buckets upstairs—tell him to replace the frozen rose ice if it's melting.'

Valentina left her staff buzzing around following instructions. Thankfully as the reception was being held in the sumptuous flagship Corretti Hotel—which was right across a verdant square from the beautiful medieval basilica where the wedding was being celebrated—she had full access to their facilities, house chefs and staff. The eponymous restaurant here was Michelin-starred, so she couldn't have asked for more. She merely had to oversee everything but was ultimately responsible for the entire menu.

Valentina found the changing area and struggled out

of her jeans and T-shirt and changed into her one smart black suit and white shirt. She surmised grimly that Carmela was far too canny to have things go wrong in the Corretti name. Far better to be able to blame an outside caterer. Valentina told herself that it was still the opportunity of a lifetime and all she had to do was make sure nothing went wrong. Simple!

After a couple of minutes she stood in her stocking feet and looked at herself in the mirror. She made a face at her flushed cheeks and the shadows under her eyes and scrabbled for her make-up bag, hands trembling from the excess adrenalin as she did her best to counteract the ravages of several sleepless nights.

She'd had nightmares of people choking on a canapé, or epidemic levels of food poisoning after the wedding lunch. The thought of felling the entire Corretti and Battaglia clans was enough to make her an insomniac for years to come! Grimacing at her far too vivid imagination, Valentina wound up her hair into a high bun at the back of her head and gave herself a quick cursory once-over. No jewellery, minimal make-up. All designed to fade as much into the background as possible. Then she gathered up her things and slipped on a pair of mid-height black court shoes.

It was only as she walking back out to the preparation area that the rogue thought slipped into her mind like a sly traitor waiting in the wings. *What if he's here?* He won't be, Valentina assured herself with something bordering uncomfortably on panic. Why would he be here when it was common knowledge he'd left home at sixteen and become completely independent of his family? The fact that he'd since carved out a stupendously successful career breeding and training thoroughbred horses had served to further that estrangement from his own family business and legacy.

He won't be here, Valentina assured herself again. Because if he was… Her mind froze as a yawning chasm of grief and pain and anger washed through her, along with something much more disturbing and hard to define.

He wouldn't be. He *couldn't* be. She was far too vulnerable today to deal with seeing Giacomo Corretti.

If there was any mercy in this world, Valentina told herself fervently, he would be kept away by the sheer psychic force of her anger and hatred. And yet, her heart beat a little faster as she went about her business.

Gio put his fingers between his bow-tied shirt and neck, trying in vain to ease the constriction he felt. He gave up with a muffled curse, leaving his white bow tie slightly askew. The problem was that the constriction was in his chest, and had nothing to do with his tie. He cursed again and wished he was on the other side of the island in his habitual uniform of T-shirt, jeans and boots, with his horses.

He could see people milling about outside the hotel and in the lush landscaped square that was between the huge imposing church and the Corretti Hotel. Clearly the wedding had ended but the luncheon hadn't started yet.

Damn. He'd almost hoped he'd be too late entirely. The only reason he'd come at all had been because his mother had pleaded with him. 'Gio, you never see your brothers, or anyone else. You can't go on isolating yourself like this. *Please* come.'

He'd had to bite back the frustration—the urge to lash out and say something like, *Why the hell should I?* But he hadn't, he'd been immediately disgusted by his own pathetic self-pity and his relationship with his mother was tenuous at the best of times.

As a young boy he'd been witness to his parents' volatile relationship and had watched as his mother had become more and more insecure and self-loathing as she'd tried in vain to keep the attention of her straying husband, Gio's deceased father. Unfortunately her growing instability and self-absorption had coincided with a particularly vulnerable time in Gio's life, and so while affection for her was there…Gio couldn't force an intimacy that had been long ago irreparably eroded.

But he was an adult now and took responsibility for his own actions; it was futile to dwell on the past. He forced his mind back to his mother: if she had some fantasy notion of bringing all of her sons under one roof for their cousin's wedding then would it really be so hard to at least put in an appearance?

So now he was here, hovering on the edge of the square. He smiled grimly at the imagery. He'd been hovering on the edges of his family for as long as he could remember. The youngest male in the Corretti dynasty. The youngest in his own family. Dominated by two older brothers who'd vied for supremacy, and a father who had been mercilessly exacting of all of his sons, not least his quietest one. The one who had disappointed him on every possible level with frailties that were unacceptable in a Corretti male.

Gio ruthlessly pushed aside the memories that threatened to rise and choke him. That way lay madness and even worse memories. Drawing on the icy veneer he'd surrounded himself with for years now, Gio pushed an impatient hand through his unruly hair. He was aware that he wasn't perhaps as clean shaven as he could be, but he just cursed softly again and strode forward and towards the towering Corretti edifice.

Valentina looked blankly at the ladder in her tights. She'd come by way of a ladder in her tights when she'd been all but knocked down by Alessandro Corretti, the groom. In-

stead of greeting a triumphant married couple after their
wedding ceremony, it had been just the groom who had
burst into the main reception room like an exploding tor-
nado. She, and a tray of delicate hors d'oeuvres had gone
flying, and with Alessandro blissfully unaware of the car-
nage left in his wake, he'd barrelled on.

As she'd scrabbled around on the ground picking up the
detritus before anyone else saw it, her assistant Sara had
appeared and bent down to help, hissing sotto voce as she
did, 'The wedding is off—the bride just jilted the groom,
right there in the church.'

Valentina had looked at her—a sick feeling blooming
in her belly. And then she'd heard the sudden flurry of
approaching hissed whispers. The stunned and shocked
guests were obviously making their way to the reception.

Before she'd had time to figure out what this all meant,
Carmela Corretti had swept into the reception hot on the
heels of her son, with a face like thunder. She'd spotted
Valentina and roughly hauled her up with a hand under
her arm. 'The wedding might be off, but you will proceed
with this reception for whoever turns up, do you hear me?'

She'd let Valentina go then and looked down that ele-
gant nose. 'As you'll be looking after less than a full guest
count, I won't be paying you for services not rendered.'

It had taken a second for her meaning to sink in and then
Valentina had gasped out loud. 'But…that's…'

Carmela had cut in ruthlessly. 'I will not discuss this
further. Now instruct your staff to tend to the guests who
do arrive. I won't have anyone say that we turned them
away.'

In shock, Valentina had done as instructed, far too
mindful of Carmela Corretti's influence should she defy
her. And as she'd watched the staff rushing around serving amongst the arriving shell-shocked guests, as if noth-

ing had just happened, Valentina had felt incredibly shaky
with reaction.

She couldn't afford to spill champagne on a haute cou-
ture gown or drop a tray into someone's lap so she'd retreated to a quiet corner for a moment to try and steady her
nerves and process this information. And the fact that Carmela wasn't going to pay her! The ladder in her tights was
the least of her worries…who on earth would now touch the
caterer associated with the wedding scandal of the year?

Gio took another full glass of champagne from a passing
waiter's tray. He'd lost count of how many he'd had but the
alcohol was having a nicely numbing effect on his brain.
He'd walked straight into the debacle of the century. Expecting to find his cousin's family jubilant and gloating
with their new merger of power, he'd instead found small
huddles of guests in the sumptuously decorated reception room, all whispering excitedly of the runaway bride.

The unfolding scandal was so unexpected that it defused
much of his simmering anger at the thought of having to
play nice with his family. He had caught a glimpse of his
older half-sister, Lia, but he'd instinctively shied away from
talking to her, never quite knowing what to say to the tall
serious woman who'd been brought up in his grandparents'
house after her mother, their father's first wife, had died.

Thinking that surely he couldn't be expected to stay
here now, Gio decided that he'd more than done his duty
and slugged back the champagne before putting the empty
glass down. He made his way out of the main function
room into the corridor and passed by an anteroom where
the wedding band were setting up and doing a sound check.
Gio shook his head in disbelief—clearly the word hadn't
reached this far yet, or perhaps his formidable aunt Car-

mela wasn't going to let a runaway bride stop her guests from dancing the night away?

Something suddenly caught Gio's peripheral vision. He stopped in his tracks. He was passing another room now, a store room. He could see that it was the figure of a woman sitting on a chair in the empty room, surrounded by boxes and other chairs piled high. Her head was down-bent, glossy chestnut hair caught up in a bun. Shapely legs under a black skirt. A white shirt and jacket. Slim pale hands clasped on her lap.

As if she could feel the weight of his gaze on her, her head started to come up. Déjà vu was so immediate and strong, Gio nearly staggered back from it. *No*, he thought, *it couldn't be her*. Not here, not now. Not ever. She was only in his dreams and nightmares. Cursing him. Along with the ghost of her brother.

But now her head was up fully and those glorious tiger eyes were widening. *It was her.* The knowledge exploded something open, deep inside him. Something that had been frozen in time for seven years. He saw colour leach from her cheeks. So much more angular now that her teenage plumpness had disappeared. *So much more beautiful.* He could see her throat work, swallowing.

She stood up with a slightly jerky move. She was taller than he remembered, slimmer and yet with very womanly curves. The promise of the burgeoning beauty that he re-membered had been truly fulfilled. So many things were impacting Gio at once that he had to shut them all down deep inside him.

He had alternately dreaded and anticipated the possibil-ity of this day for a long time. He couldn't crumble now in front of her. He wouldn't allow himself the luxury.

He walked to the entrance of the room and totally redundantly he said, 'Valentina.' And then after a pause, 'It's good to see you.'

Valentina was in shock. More shock heaped on top of shock. Without even realising she was speaking out loud she said, 'You're not meant to be here.' *The sheer force of my will should have kept you away.* But she didn't say that.

Gio's mouth turned up on one corner in a tiny movement that wasn't quite a smile, 'Well, my cousin is, *was*, the groom so I have some right to be here.' He frowned slightly. 'What are you doing here?'

Valentina's brain wasn't working properly. She answered almost absently, 'I'm the caterer.'

Gio was so much taller and broader than she remembered. Any hint of boyishness was gone. He was all stark angles and sinuous muscle and power. The suit hugged his muscular frame like a second skin. The white shirt and white bow tie made him look even darker.

His hair was still messy though, giving him a familiar devil-may-care look that rang bells somewhere dimly in Valentina's consciousness. His eyes were a light brown and a wicked voice whispered that she knew very well they could look green in certain lights.

She used to watch him and her brother for hours as they'd egged each other on in a series of daredevil stunts, either on horseback or on the mud bikes Gio had had first on his father's property, and then later, on his own property. But by then they'd been proper adult motorbikes and he and her brother had relished their death-defying races. She remembered the way Gio would tip his head back and laugh; he'd looked so vitally masculine, his teeth gleaming whitely in his face.

She remembered turning fifteen and seeing him again for the first time in about four years, because he'd been living abroad in France, building up his equine business. He'd returned home a conquering hero, a self-made millionaire, with a bevy of champion thoroughbred horses. But that had had nothing to do with how she'd instantly had an altogether different awareness of him. Her belly would twist when she saw him, and then there were the butterflies, so violent it was like feeling sick. Her gaze had been shamefully captivated by his tall rangy body.

Much to her everlasting mortification she'd tagged along on her brother's visits to Gio in his new home near Syracuse whenever he'd been home from college, during his long summers off. Gio had bought a palatial *castello* complete with a farm, where he'd installed a state-of-the-art stud and gallops. He'd been in the process of doing up a nearby run-down racetrack which by today had become the famed Corretti racetrack where the eponymous internationally renowned annual Corretti Cup race was held.

Gio had caught her staring once and she'd been so mortified she'd been red for a week. She hadn't been able to get out of her head how he'd held her gaze for a long moment, a slow smile turning up his mouth, as if something illicit and secret had passed between them. Something that scared her as much as it had exhilarated her.

He had a beautiful face, sculpted lips. High cheekbones and a hard slashing line of a nose. A strong chin. But something in his demeanour took away any prettiness. A dark brooding energy surrounded him like a force-field.

Gio lifted a hand to point to her hair and said, 'You have something…just there.' It shattered her memories and brought her back to the present. He was pointing above her right ear and Valentina reached up and felt something wet and sticky and took her hand down to see a lump of viscous orange salmon caviar.

And then it was as if the deep baritone reality of his

voice made the bells ring loud and clear in her head. He looked devil-may-care because that's what he was, and that attitude had led directly to her brother's death. For the past few moments she'd been protecting herself from the reality that he was here, in front of her, and now that protection was ripped away.

She remembered. And with that knowledge came the pain. The memories. That lonely grave in the graveyard. Seven years of an ache that didn't seem to get any better, only fade slightly. Until it caught you unawares and the wound was reopened all over again. Like right now.

How dared he stand there and talk to her as if nothing had happened? As if civility could hide the ugly past. Anger and something much darker bubbled up inside Valentina. A kind of guilt, for having remembered another time for a moment; disgusted with herself she strode out of the room and straight up to Gio. She clenched the hand that held the remnants of the once-perfect canapé and looked up at him, focusing on the blazing incinerating anger of grief, and not something much more dangerous in her belly when she realised how tall he was. 'Get out of my way, Corretti.'

Gio flinched minutely as if she'd slapped him. He could remember in vivid recall how it had felt that day when she'd punched him in the chest. And he welcomed it now. For a few seconds when she'd looked stunned and not angry, he'd thought that perhaps, with time, a mellowing had taken place. But then he mocked himself—the pain of losing Mario still as fresh as it had been on the night he died. And the shock to cushion that blow had long gone. Now there was just the excoriating and ever-present guilt.

Valentina was looking up at him, her eyes glowing gold and spitting. She hated him. It was in every taut and tense line of her body.

She gritted out, 'I said get out of my way, Corretti.'

CHAPTER TWO

GIO STEPPED BACK, his voice was stiff. 'I'm not in your way, Valentina.'

Valentina didn't move though. She was vibrating all over with anger. It was like a tangible thing.

'You need to go. You need to leave this place.'

A small flare of anger which he had no right to feel raced up Gio's spine. His mouth tightened. 'As this is my cousin's wedding I think I have a right to stay.' He didn't bother to mention he'd been about to leave.

'The wedding is off, or hadn't you heard?' Valentina supplied with a measure of satisfaction.

Something Gio didn't understand made him bullishly stand his ground. 'The reception is still on, or hadn't *you* heard?'

He saw her face pale and instinctively put out a hand to touch her but she flinched backwards, disgust etched all over her. 'Don't touch me. And yes, I know the reception is still on—half a reception, that is, which your aunt expects me to cater for without handing over one euro in payment. Your whole family are poison, Corretti, right to the core.'

Gio wanted to say, *Stop calling me that,* but instead he frowned and said, 'What do you mean? She's not paying you?'

'No,' Valentina spat out, hating that she'd blurted that

out, or that she was still even in a conversation with Giacomo Corretti.

'But that's ridiculous, you should to get paid regardless.'

Valentina laughed harshly and forced herself to look
at Gio. 'Yes, call me old-fashioned but it is customary to
be paid for services rendered. However, your aunt seems
to feel that in light of the unfortunate turn of events, she's
absolved of the duty of payment.'

'That's crazy…' Gio raked a hand through his hair, fire
entering his belly. He was fixing on something, anything,
he could do by way of helping Valentina and he knew it.
The anger at his aunt's heavy-handed and bullying tactics
was a very easy target to focus on.

He started to stride back towards the main function
room and then he heard behind him, 'Wait! Where do you
think you're going?'

Gio turned around. The sight of Valentina standing just
feet away with a stray lock of glossy silky hair caressing
one hot cheek sent something molten right into his gut.
He was shocked all over again that it was her, *here*, and
he was captivated, momentarily forgetting everything.

He felt as if he'd been existing in a fog and had suddenly
been plunged into an icy pool. Everything was bright and
piercingly clear, the sound check of the band nearby almost painful in its intensity.

And something was happening in his body. After five
years of strict sensory denial, it, too, was surging to life.
Blood was rushing to every vein and artery. *Becoming
hard.*

Valentina was oblivious to this cataclysm going on in
Gio's body. She pointed a finger at him. 'I asked you where
you think you're going?'

Gio sucked in a breath and felt dizzy—as if someone
had just spiked the air around him with a mind-altering

drug. He struggled to focus on what she'd asked and not on the lush curve of her mouth, the perfect bow of its shape. He hadn't even been noticing women for so long and now this—it was like an overload on his senses.

'My aunt…' he managed finally, focusing carefully on the words. 'My aunt, I'll tell her she can't do this to you.'

He turned again, as much to put some distance between himself and Valentina as anything else but wasn't prepared for when a hand gripped his arm, pulling him around. She was suddenly too close. Gio all but reeled back and Valentina dropped her hand and looked him up and down scathingly. 'You're drunk.'

He could have laughed. He knew very well that after the shock of seeing this woman again he was no more drunk than she was.

Gio forced control on his wayward body, but he was tingling all over. He still felt the touch of her hand like a brand.

'I'll go to my aunt and tell her she—'

'No, you won't,' Valentina interjected hotly. 'You'll do no such thing. I do not need you to fight my battles for me, Corretti.'

Something snapped inside Gio and he gritted his jaw. 'It's *Gio*, or have you forgotten you once called me that?'

Valentina's face was carved from stone. 'No, I haven't forgotten, but apparently you've forgotten why I'd never call you that again.'

The cruelty of that statement nearly felled Gio but he stayed standing. 'No,' he said faintly, 'I haven't forgotten.'

Their eyes were locked, amber with hazel. For a moment there was nothing but simmering emotion between them, so strong and tangible that when one of the band members started to walk out of the room they'd been rehearsing in, he took one look at the couple locked in silent combat and retreated back inside, closing the door softly.

'I'll pay you—I'll cover whatever my aunt should be paying you.'

Valentina reared back, her hands curled into tiny fists, two spots of hectic colour on her white cheeks. *'You?'*

Gio steeled himself.

'I wouldn't take your filthy money if it was offered to me on a silver platter.'

Of course, he conceded bitterly, she would have nothing to do with him, or his money, no matter how hard he'd worked for it.

Valentina pointed a finger at her chest then and Gio swallowed hard and fought not to let his eyes drop to those provocative swells underneath the plain white shirt. 'I am a professional and I've been hired to do a job and that's what I'm going to do. I will not let your aunt jeopardise my reputation by running out now. And I will not take your guilt money, Corretti.'

Guilt money. The words fell on him hard. This time Gio didn't correct her use of his name. For the first time he saw the bright sheen of tears in her eyes and something inside him broke apart. The memory of her stoic back that day by the graveside was vivid. But he couldn't move or say a thing. She wouldn't welcome it.

Suddenly the doors to the main function room opened and a young girl appeared with a worried face beside them. 'Val, *there* you are. We need you inside, *now.* Mrs Corretti is looking for you.'

Valentina's chin came up but she looked at Gio. 'Thanks, Sara, I'll be in in a second.'

She waited until the girl had left and then she said to Gio with icy emphasis, 'I think the least you can do is leave. And I sincerely hope never to have to see you again.'

And then she walked by him, giving him a wide berth as if afraid to even come close to touching him. Gio heard the doors open and close behind him. Her scent lingered on the air, light and musky. *Her.*

I think the least you can do is leave. Gio hadn't needed much of an excuse before. And he certainly didn't need one now. The past seven years had just fallen away like the flimsiest of sets on a stage to expose all of the ugliness and pain that was still there.

As much as Valentina never wanted to see him again, he echoed that sentiment right at that moment. He didn't think he could survive another encounter with her.

A week later...

'*Who* did you say?' Gio's voice rang with incredulity. Was he hearing things? He shook his head and focused again on his PA, a comfortably middle-aged woman called Agata.

She spoke again slowly, enunciating every word carefully. 'Val-en-tina Ferr-anti. She's outside right now, she wants to see you. And she looks determined.'

Gio turned his back on Agata for a moment and spiked two hands through his already messy hair, his whole body knotting with tension and something much hotter, darker. Already he could feel blood pooling southwards. His mouth tightened. So it hadn't been an aberration. It was her, uniquely her, who was having this effect on him.

Perfetto. His body and libido were being awoken by the only woman in the world he could never have. Or more accurately who would never have *him.*

He turned around again, hiding his tumultuous thoughts behind an impassive expression. Valentina would not affect him today. She'd obviously just come to hurl a few more

spiked arrows in his direction and he would withstand it
if it killed him. It was his due.

'Send her in.'

Valentina's hands were clammy, and she smoothed them
again on her worn jeans. She resolutely pushed down the
memory of the words she'd hurled at Gio Corretti just days
ago: *I wouldn't take your filthy money if it was offered to
me on a silver platter.* Her cheeks got hot with guilt.

What was taking his assistant so long? Perhaps she
should have dressed up more? Instead of these old jeans,
sneakers and a T-shirt that had definitely seen better days.
Too late now. And anyway, it wasn't as if she was trying
to impress Giacomo Corretti. She was only here because
he was literally the only person on the island of Sicily outside the sphere of his aunt's influence.

Even though Valentina knew that Gio had built up a successful business, she'd been surprised when she'd come
to his offices at his racetrack in Syracuse—to find everything so pristine and gleaming. She wasn't sure what she'd
expected, some level of obvious debauchery?

For a couple of years after Mario's death, Gio Corretti
became the most hedonistic playboy in Europe. Always
a lover of extreme sports, he'd seemed to relish doing as
many dangerous things as possible. He'd been pictured
jumping out of planes, rock climbing with his bare hands,
scaling the highest mountains in the world.

He'd also been pictured on yachts in the south of France,
in the casinos of Monte Carlo and in the winners' enclo-
sures at Epsom and Longchamp, where he'd regularly won
and lost millions of euros in the space of hours. And in
each place a stunning woman on his arm, clinging to him
with besotted adoration and euro signs in her eyes.

But contrary to that feckless image, his racetrack was a

veritable hive of industry with smartly turned-out grooms wearing black T-shirts emblazoned with the Corretti Racetrack logo, leading sleek-looking thoroughbreds through the grounds, and gardeners tending the lushly flowering borders.

The most impressive part of the location was the racetrack which overlooked the Mediterranean Sea, giving it a vista unlike any other in the world. This wasn't where Mario had died—Valentina didn't think she could have come here today if it was. Mario had died on the smaller training gallops at Gio's *castello*, because this racetrack hadn't yet been ready.

Valentina heard the low hum of voices in Gio's office where the friendly middle-aged lady had disappeared moments before and her belly knotted. Anger at seeing Gio again had been her impetus through this horrific week and the spectacular implosion of her career—anger is what had impelled her here because one Corretti had ruined her but only another Corretti could save her—but what if he was telling his assistant that he didn't want to see her?

Just then she heard a sound like the door handle jiggling and she flinched and stood up, her heart thumping at the thought of seeing Gio again. What had she been thinking? She couldn't do this. She was in the act of turning to leave when she heard a calm mellifluous voice announce, 'Sorry to keep you waiting, Ms Ferranti, he'll see you now.'

Gio's body was locked tight as he waited for Valentina to appear in the doorway and when she did, in jeans and a T-shirt, with her hair loose over her shoulders in chestnut waves, a whole new tension came into his body.

Her T-shirt was moulded over the firm globes of her breasts. Gio felt like he couldn't breathe and dragged his gaze back up to those feline amber eyes. The same eyes that had been haunting him all week.

He put out a hand and said stiffly, 'Please, won't you sit down?'

Valentina hovered uncertainly just inside the door, which Agata had closed behind her on her way out. She shook her head. 'No, I'd prefer to stand.'

Gio inclined his head and stayed behind his desk, as if that could offer some protection.

Valentina crossed her arms then, inadvertently pushing her breasts together and up, and Gio nearly groaned out loud. He cursed himself—he was acting like a hormonal teenager.

More tersely than he intended, he rapped out, 'You'll have to forgive me for being a little surprised to see you. After all, it was hardly your intention the last time we met.'

Valentina found herself floundering, badly. Seeing Gio again last week, her response then had been visceral and a reflex to years-old grief and anger. After all, she hadn't seen him since the funeral. But now that raw emotion was stripped away somewhat and left in its place was something much more ambiguous. And a physical awareness of the man which was very disturbing.

A huge window behind him looked out over the racing ground and stands, the sea beyond. But Valentina could only see him in a dark polo shirt which was stretched across a hard muscled chest, and long, long legs clad in lovingly worn jeans. Without even looking properly she could imagine his thighs—like powerful columns of sheer muscle.

When he and Mario had been on horseback they'd been a sight to behold, but Gio even more so. He'd moved with such fluid grace that it had been hard to tell where he ended and the horse began. Her brother hadn't had such an innate ability.… Valentina gulped. She couldn't think of that now.

She struggled to recall his words, something about her not wanting to see him again. Her throat felt scratchy. 'No…it wasn't my intention.'

One of Gio's black brows arched. 'And it is now?'

Valentina cursed herself for ever thinking of this as a plan of action and tried desperately to articulate herself. 'Yes. Well, it's just that…things have happened in the past week.'

Gio came around his desk then and perched on the corner, legs outstretched before him. His scent tantalised Valentina's nostrils and just like that she was flung back in time to when she'd turned seventeen, weeks before Mario's death. She'd taken her moped to Gio's *castello* to look for Mario for their father, who'd needed him to do chores. In those days Valentina hadn't needed any excuse to go to Gio's *castello* or the track.

She'd gone to the stables looking for Mario and had seen no one, aware that she was disappointed not to see Gio either. And then a horse had appeared out of nowhere behind her. A huge beast. Valentina had jumped back, startled, ashamed of how intimidated she was around horses.

Someone had come up behind her and before she knew what was happening she'd been lifted effortlessly onto the horse's bare back, and Gio had been swinging himself up behind her, an arm snug around her waist, thighs hard around hers. She'd been so shocked to find herself that high off the ground and with Gio in such close proximity that she'd struggled for breath as terror and excitement had constricted her lungs.

He'd said in her ear, 'You'll never get comfortable with horses if you don't get used to riding them.'

He'd put the reins in her hands with his hands over hers and for about half an hour they'd walked around his sandy gallops with Gio murmuring words of encouragement and tuition in her ears. Terror had turned to exhilaration as she'd allowed herself to relax into Gio's protective embrace and when her brother had still failed to materialise Gio had told her that he'd left before she'd arrived, borrowing one of Gio's collection of motorbikes to get home.

Valentina had all but slithered off the horse and on very shaky legs had fled home herself. Mortified to think they'd been entirely alone for all that time. She'd been unable to look at Gio for weeks afterwards without blushing, achingly aware of how her whole body had tingled next to his, and how hot she'd felt between her legs.

'What things?'

Valentina looked blankly at Gio now, her mind still dazed from the memory.

'You said things have happened?'

Valentina came crashing back to earth. Why on earth was she remembering such traitorous memories when only one was important? The memory of when she and her parents had rushed into that hospital in Palermo only to be stopped by a doctor and told that their son was dead.

Valentina focused on that now and crossed her arms even tighter across her chest. This man owed her. Owed her parents. Owed her brother. 'Your aunt refused to pay me for the catering at the wedding.'

Gio frowned. 'Did you tell her you wouldn't accept non-payment?'

Valentina flushed. She'd been so angry and emotional after seeing Gio that when she'd come face to face with Carmela Corretti and the woman had still refused to pay her even though people were sitting down to the six-course meal, despite the shambles of the wedding, that she'd threatened legal action.

Even now Valentina could almost laugh at the folly of her naivety! As if a mere mortal like her could take on a Corretti. Carmela had looked at her and her face had gone white and then red with anger at this impudence.

'You dare to threaten me with legal action.'

Hands on hips, gone too far to back down now, Valentina had fumed. 'Yes, I do. You don't scare me, you know.'

Carmela had just smiled and said as if she were remarking on the weather, 'You can consider yourself not only not paid, Ms Ferranti, you can also consider yourself blacklisted from every catering job on this island. I did warn you, did I not?'

Valentina had gasped at the unfairness of this attack. 'But there's nothing wrong with the menu or the catering service.'

'No,' agreed Carmela almost cheerfully. 'But, there is everything wrong with you and your attitude, young lady.'

That had been too much for Valentina, to be spoken to so patronisingly by a Corretti. She'd seen an ice bucket nearby full of water and her hands had itched to pour it over the woman's head. But she'd been saved from that impetuous action when the abandoned groom had reappeared and suddenly Carmela had pushed Valentina out of the way to go to him.

Gio said nothing for a long moment and then, 'I think I would have paid to see my aunt with a full ice bucket over her head.'

Valentina snuck a look at Gio's expression. And then as she watched, his eyes sparkled and his mouth twitched. It was so unexpected to see this, that to her horror, Valentina could feel a lightness bubbling up inside herself too.

No! her brain screamed. *Do not let him close, do not let him charm you.*

Fighting the lightness down with an iron will Valentina suddenly realised that she'd been totally and utterly wrong to come here. Had she come because seeing Gio last week had precipitated a dangerous need to see him again? The very thought of such a susceptibility made her feel nauseous.

Without even thinking about it, she'd whirled around to the door and had her hand on the handle before she felt a much larger hand around her upper arm, tugging her back. That touch sent tremors of sensation and *wanting* into her blood. She had to leave now.

She pulled her arm free and looked up at Gio, who was too close. 'I made a mistake coming here.'

All lightness was gone from Gio now; his eyes were flashing green, his mouth was tight. 'You hardly came all the way here from Palermo for nothing, Valentina.'

She shook her head, feeling sick. Memories were coming up too thick and fast, jumbling everything up, when she had to remember why she hated this man. 'I shouldn't have come. I thought you could help me with something but I forgot—I don't want…*need* your help.'

And then she yanked the door open and ran all the way out of his building and didn't stop till she got to her rusty old car.

Gio slammed the door shut after Valentina left and put his two hands against it and dropped his head. 'Damn, damn, *damn.*'

That evening when Valentina got home from checking on her parents she paced the floor of her tiny spartan apartment. Things were not good. Her father hadn't looked well at all, pasty and slightly sweaty, but he'd brushed aside her concerns. Worry knotted Valentina's insides. She hadn't told them yet of the debacle of her career which had effectively been ruined by Carmela Corretti. Between her parents—with her father's ominous chest pains and her mother's arthritis and only access to the most basic health care—it was a serious worry.

She stopped pacing and put a weary hand to her head. She *had* to work. But thanks to Carmela she'd be lucky to get a job as a chambermaid in a three-star hotel in Messina. And that wasn't all—her two staff were also unemployed thanks to her impetuous actions.

Valentina sat down on a rickety chair and cursed herself soundly. Why did she have to get so emotional and react to Carmela like that?

Gio. Because seeing him had pushed her over the edge. Had made her reckless and had brought up all the simmering anger at the Correttis in general for their lavish and effortlessly powerful ways. The way they didn't have to think of anyone but themselves.

But Valentina's conscience smote her—Gio hadn't always been like the others. He'd been shy and quiet. Withdrawn. Her father had worked doing odd jobs and maintenance for the Corretti palazzo near Palermo all his life and her mother had done their laundry. They'd lived in a tiny humble house nearby.

At first Gio and Mario hadn't been friends—they'd circled each other for a long time like two suspicious animals. Valentina had witnessed how their friendship had bonded after a particularly nasty fight. She'd been just five and had been trailing her beloved father and brother as she usually did, in awe of the palazzo and its extensive grounds. Mario had been goading Gio with fists raised. 'Come on, say something, why don't you? Don't you have a tongue?'

From her hiding place, Valentina had seen how Gio

had launched himself at Mario with a feral grunt. Her father had found them and taken both boys by the scruffs of their necks and ordered them to apologise to each other.

She'd watched as Gio had struggled to get the words out, his face smeared with dirt and dust. It had been excruciating to watch. 'I…I…I'm…s-s-s-s…' He'd stopped and then tried again, eventually saying 'sorry' in a rush.

She could remember the look on his face, as if he'd been waiting for Mario to laugh or make fun of him. He had a stutter. That's why he never spoke. Even though she'd only been five, Valentina had been aware of her ten-year-old brother's sheer maturity and grace when he'd ignored Gio's debilitating stutter and had held out his hand and said, 'I'm sorry too.'

Since that day they'd been inseparable. Valentina fought against this memory, much as she'd fought against the ones earlier—she didn't want to remember Gio like that.

Her hands clenched to fists. If Mario hadn't been so in thrall to Gio, he would never have put aside his studies that night and gone to Gio's *castello* to race horses with him. She could remember the conversation when Gio had turned up on his motorbike to entice Mario away. Mario had protested. 'I really should be studying for my exams.'

Gio had made a face. 'That's the lamest excuse I ever heard, Ferranti.'

Mario had chuckled and then said teasingly, 'Well, at least some of us *want* to get an education!'

Gio had growled at that and had launched himself at Mario and the two had mock fought for a few minutes. Valentina had been watching all of this surreptitiously from behind the door, her eyes glued in fascination to Gio's lean muscular form. Then they'd stopped and Mario had stood back breathing heavily, a dangerous glint in his eye that

Valentina recognised all too well. 'I'll come if you let me ride Black Star.'

Immediately Valentina had tensed and looked at Gio, who was scowling. 'No way, Mario…you know I won't let you near him—he's too dangerous.'

Mario had taunted, 'You're saying you're the *only* one who can handle him?'

Gio had flushed and Valentina had leapt out of her hiding place to stand between the young men, looking at Gio. 'Don't let him near that horse, Gio. I swear to God—'

Her brother had taken her shoulders and gently moved her out of the way, saying, 'This is none of your concern, Val.'

But Valentina had implored Gio with her eyes. She'd seen Black Star in action on his gallops. He was a mythically huge thoroughbred that Gio had bought recently in France. He was very controversial because while he had the potential to be a great champion, he'd already run a few races and in each one had unseated his jockey. In one tragic instance, the jockey had been killed.

The authorities in Europe had wanted to put the horse down but Gio had stepped in to buy him, claiming that he could tame him into acquiescence, putting forward the argument that the horse shouldn't be punished for the failure of the trainers. But when Gio had shown the horse off to Mario and her when he'd returned home, she'd seen a madness in his eyes that had terrified her. So far, the only one who'd been able to get near him was Gio. And now her brother wanted a go?

There'd been a stand-off between the two men. Mario had cajoled, 'Gio…come on.'

Gio had just looked at Mario for a long moment and then shrugged lightly and said, 'We'll see.'

Mario had grinned in triumph and clapped his friend on the shoulder, saying, 'Wait here, I'll just change.'

He'd left and Gio had looked at Valentina, causing that inevitable self-conscious flush to rise up through her whole body. She ignored it. 'Gio…you can't let him near that horse…something will happen to him. You know he's not as good as you.'

Gio had come close and touched his finger to Valentina's chin, tipping it up slightly, making her heart beat fast and her body ache with a peculiar restlessness.

'Don't worry, *piccolina*, I won't let anything happen to him.'

Indignant fire had raced up Valentina's spine and she'd jerked her chin free. 'Don't call me that, I'm not little.'

Gio had said nothing for a long moment, just looked at her so intensely that she'd felt breathless, and then in a slightly rougher tone of voice, 'I know you're not…and don't worry. I'll have him back to his boring books before midnight, just like Cinderella.'

Mario had reappeared and gave Valentina a hug and walked out the door, Gio had followed with a quick glance backwards. *'Ciao, bellissima.'*

And that had been the last time she'd seen Mario. When she'd seen Gio in the hospital later that night she'd run to him, distraught, hysterical. 'You let him go on that horse, didn't you, *didn't you*?'

Gio had just stood there, white-faced, and said, 'I'm so sorry.'

Her mother and father had been so proud of Mario. Everything, all of their hopes and fears, had rested on him. Valentina had resigned herself to the fact that she wouldn't have the same opportunities. She was genuinely happy for her brother to succeed and he'd often told her, 'Val, when I become a lawyer and I'm making lots of money, I'll send you to a cordon bleu school in France....'

Tears pricked her eyes, but just then a knock came on Valentina's apartment door, wrenching her back to the present. Surprised, because she wasn't used to visitors, she dashed away the dampness on her cheeks and stood up. When she opened the door and saw who it was she sucked in a breath. *'You.'*

CHAPTER THREE

Gio looked grim in the dim light of the corridor. 'Yes, it's me.'

Still too shocked to make much sense of this she just said, 'How did you get up here?' The front door was at ground level and there were five apartments in the ancient crumbling building which was on one of Palermo's less salubrious streets.

'Someone was coming in just as I arrived.'

'How did you know where I lived?'

Gio's mouth tightened. 'I asked around.'

Valentina could just bet he had—and who wouldn't give a Corretti the information they wanted? Seeing him here like this in the flesh when she'd just been feeling so vulnerable made Valentina prickly.

'What do you want, Gio?' She saw the flash in his eyes and realised she'd just called him *Gio*. Flutters erupted in her belly.

'I'd like to come in for a minute if that's OK?'

'No, it's not OK.'

Valentina started to close the door but was surprised when she felt the resistance of Gio's hand. Suddenly he looked quite intimidating.

'We can conduct this conversation here in the doorway

and give your neighbours something to listen to or you can invite me in.'

Valentina heard the tell-tale creak of her neighbour's door just then and very reluctantly let Gio come in. He went and stood in the middle of the small living area, which had the kitchen area just off it and a tiny bedroom and bathroom on the other side. Palatial it was not, especially when she thought about his *castello*.

She smiled with saccharine sweetness. 'Well, I don't think you're here for tips on how to live in a small space.'

A corner of his mouth turned up and the flutters in Valentina's belly intensified. Damn him.

'No. That's not why I'm here.' He turned to face her then and she noticed that he'd changed out of his polo shirt and jeans, into a white shirt and chinos. His overlong hair curled over his collar, a lock falling near his eyes.

'I'm here because you ran out today after saying you didn't need me to help you. But clearly you were prepared to ask for help up until that point. You wouldn't have driven across the island for nothing.'

Valentina cursed herself again for having gone to him at all. She lifted her chin. 'It was a bad idea. Everything is fine.'

Gio crossed his arms. 'I know my aunt Carmela—I'd imagine that everything is not fine at all.'

Valentina's belly lurched. Things weren't fine. They were awful. But she wouldn't ask Gio for help. She *couldn't*. There was too much history between them. Along with all sorts of dangerous undercurrents she didn't want to look at. *So,* a small voice asked her now, *so why did you go to him today*?

Firmly Valentina opened her door again and stood aside. She looked at Gio but avoided his eyes. 'I shouldn't have gone to you today. I'd like you to leave *now*.'

Gio looked at the woman standing so stiffly by the door and wanted to shake her. She'd come today for *something*. Exasperated now he said, 'Look, Valentina, you know you can talk to me. You can tell me whatever it is, if you need something.'

She looked at him then and for the first time he noticed that she was pale and she looked tired, shadows under her eyes. Worry on her face.

'No, *you* look. Pretend you never saw me today. Now for the second time, I'd like you to leave. You shouldn't have come all the way here.'

'Valentina, for crying out loud—' Gio broke off when a shrill ring pierced the tense atmosphere. He looked down and could see a mobile vibrating on the small coffee table. Automatically he bent to pick it up and saw that it said, *Home*. His gut clenched. Valentina's parents. He handed it to her, saying, 'It's your—'

But she cut him off. 'I know who it is.'

She took the phone and turned her back to him saying, 'Mama?'

Gio's gaze travelled down over the glossy hair in messy waves over shoulders and slender back and then his eyes went to the rounded curve of her bottom. He wanted to walk up to her and pull her hair aside and press a kiss to the side of her neck. He wanted to encircle her waist with his arm, and feel the brush of her breasts on his skin. He wanted to pull her back into his body, moulding her to him. Instantly his body responded with a wave of heat. The sudden need was so intense he shook with it.

It was a few seconds before he noticed that Valentina had turned and was looking at him, her face pale and stricken. Immediately he was alert, eyes narrowed on her. 'What is it?'

'My father has collapsed.'

Gio was moving before she'd even finished speaking and they were outside and in his car a few seconds after that. Valentina rattled off the address. Luckily she didn't live far from her parents, who had moved into Palermo after her father had retired from working at the Corretti palazzo.

They pulled up outside the modest house and Valentina was out of the car and through the front door when Gio got out of the car. He followed her in, an awful hollow feeling in his belly. If anything happened to her father... Just then he saw the man on the floor, his face white. Valentina's mother was sobbing over the body and he could see Valentina starting to shake violently.

Gio came in and gently moved Valentina aside and then in cool authoritative tones instructed her to call an ambulance. While she was on the phone he knelt down beside Emilio Ferranti and listened for a heartbeat and heard nothing.

Expertly Gio opened the man's shirt and started CPR. He felt someone pulling his arm and saw Valentina's face, white with worry and shock. 'What are you doing?'

Gio shrugged her off gently but firmly. 'I'm giving him CPR.' And then he bent to his task and didn't look up until the paramedics arrived and pulled him to one side. He was breathing fast and sweating as he watched them hook Emilio up to various things. Then they put him on a gurney and wheeled him into the ambulance, with Valentina's mother getting into the back. One of the paramedics was talking to Valentina, and then they were gone with the ambulance lights flashing and the siren wailing intermittently.

Gio went up to Valentina. She looked at him, dazed. His heart turned over in his chest. 'Come on, I'll take you to the hospital.'

He led her to the car and put her in, fastening the safety belt around her when she made no move to do so.

When they were on the road with the lights of the ambulance just visible in the far distance he felt her turn to him. 'The paramedic told me you probably saved his life. I…I didn't know what you were doing.'

Gio shrugged minutely. 'Don't worry about it, it can look scary.'

'Where did you learn to do that?'

A bleakness entered Gio and he didn't say, *I learnt how to do it after Mario died, when I couldn't save him, or help him.* Instead he just said lightly, 'I run a business—I insist that all my staff have basic first aid training, including myself.' Gio's experience was a bit more than just in first aid, he'd actually done a paramedic training course. The way he'd felt so helpless next to Mario's inert body had forged within him a strong desire never to feel that helpless again. The awful thing was that Mario had been alive for a while, but Gio hadn't known how to keep him alive. And he'd died in Gio's arms before the medics had arrived.

'I…thank you.'

Gio winced. 'You don't have to say anything.'

The rest of the journey was made in silence and when they got to the hospital Gio pushed down the awful sense of déjà vu. The night of Mario's accident, he'd hoped against hope that somehow miraculously they'd brought Mario back to life but when he'd got there he'd seen the small huddle of Valentina with her parents, crying. Valentina had rushed at him with her fists flying. 'I knew something would happen. You shouldn't have taken him out. He wouldn't have gone if you'd not asked him….'

The memory faded, to be replaced now by the frantic chaos of the emergency room. Valentina went and asked at the desk and then, with a quick glance at Gio, who just nodded at her, she disappeared with a nurse.

Gio made a phone call like an automaton to one of his staff to come and switch his impractical sports car for something more practical. It was shortly after that had been delivered when he saw the bowed figure of Valentina's mother, with Valentina all but holding her up. *Please God*, he prayed silently.

But when they got close Valentina looked at him and smiled tiredly. 'He's stable. It was a massive heart attack and the doctor said if he hadn't been given CPR he wouldn't have made it.'

Gio felt uncomfortable and just said, 'I have a car outside, let me take you home.'

Valentina's mother acknowledged Gio but to his relief she didn't seem too upset to see him there, or surprised. He solicitously helped them into the jeep that had been delivered and then Valentina said, 'You can take us to my mother's. I'll stay with her tonight.'

When Gio pulled up outside the house again he jumped out to help Valentina's mother. At the door she stopped and looked up at him. 'Thank you, Gio.'

He looked into her lined and careworn face and couldn't see anything but tired gratitude. She patted his hand and then went inside the house. When Valentina was about to pass him he stopped her with a hand on her arm. She looked at him and he had to curb his response to her.

'If you need anything...*anything* at all, you know where to find me. I mean it, Valentina.'

She started to say, 'I...' and then she stopped and said, 'OK.' And then she went inside and closed the door.

A week after he'd left Valentina at her mother's house, Gio was trying not to think of her and was looking at a picture in the local newspaper. A huge headline was proclaiming: Scandals in the Corretti Family! There was a salacious rumour that the runaway bride had actually run away with his older brother Matteo after the non-wedding. And it had been revealed that his cousin, Rosa, was not actually his cousin but another half-sister, thanks to an affair between his aunt Carmela and his father.

Gio's mouth twisted in disgust. He wanted nothing to do with the sordid details of these stories. He did feel a twinge of sympathy for Rosa, who had always been quite sweet to him on the rare occasions they'd met. He could imagine that this must be devastating news to deal with....

Gio's phone rang at that moment and it was a number he didn't recognise. Unconsciously his insides tensed. He threw down the paper and picked the phone up. *'Pronto?'*

There was nothing for a few seconds and then *her* voice came down the line. 'It's me.'

Gio's belly tightened. Carefully he said, 'How is your father?'

Valentina sounded weary. 'He's doing OK, still in hospital, but it looks like he needs a major bypass operation.'

There was another long silence and then, 'Gio…I…'

Gio clutched the phone, suddenly feeling panicky. *If she hangs up…* 'Go on, Valentina, what is it?'

He heard her sigh audibly and then she said, 'I need you to give me a job.'

'I don't have any formal training—I'll work in the kitchen…I'll work wherever you want.'

Gio schooled his expression, but his chest tightened at the pride in Valentina's voice. She'd come to him today, the day after she'd phoned, dressed in black slacks and a white shirt. Hair tied back in a low ponytail. Face pale. Avoiding his eyes. She must hate this.

Something piqued his curiosity. 'Where *did* you train?'

Valentina looked at him then and he had to keep an even more rigid control on his control.

'You remember my nonna?'

Gio nodded. He had a vague memory of their grandmother, a small woman with sparkling brown eyes. She'd been at the grave that day too, a wizened matriarch who should never have had to see her grandson buried before her. Gio fought down the predictable tightness in his chest, and Valentina continued. 'She was a cook for a local trattoria, and she was my first teacher. From when I was tiny she taught me all the basics and her secrets. When I left school I went to work with her, and then when she passed away, I worked for Marcel Picheron as a commis-chef.'

Her mouth twisted minutely. 'My parents had pooled all their resources into—' She stopped abruptly and the name hung silently in the air like an accusation—*Mario*. Then she looked away for a moment before continuing through the thick tension in the air. 'They had no more money to send me to college, but I heard about Marcel's open days when he would audition unknowns so I auditioned and got in.'

Gio remembered well how Mario's parents had put every cent into his education. And yet Valentina had never shown any signs of being bitter about her own education being neglected. She'd been as proud as they had.

He could only imagine how good Valentina must have been to impress the cantankerous old French chef who had more Michelin stars than any other chef in Italy and who ran the most exclusive restaurant on the island. It had a waiting list of six months.

Valentina glanced at Gio again. 'I worked my way up to sous-chef but I found that my forte was in devising menus and creating hors d'oeuvres.'

Dryly he remarked now, 'You probably have had a better training than most people out of a cordon bleu school in Paris.'

Valentina shrugged, her cheeks going pink. 'I set up my own catering company with two friends a year ago. We come up with menus for events, and then we hire outside chefs to come in and cook. I make all the canapés. In general I supervise everything, and step in to chef if I need to.'

Gio recalled the small part of the reception he'd seen a few weeks ago. He could remember the intricately delicate canapés, how appetising and original they'd looked even though he'd had no appetite for them, his gut too churned up to be there in the first place.

He got up from behind his desk and stood at the huge window with hands in his pockets, observing but not really seeing the hive of activity out on the racecourse. He turned back to face Valentina, who was sitting in a chair. She looked as delicate and brittle as spun glass.

'The annual Corretti Cup race meeting is coming up in three weeks. It runs for three days with the Corretti Cup race on the last day. We provide a full entertainment package here, including a set menu for lunch every day. I'd like you to come up with the menu for that main luncheon each day, and also look after catering for the evening champagne receptions.'

His words took a minute to sink in. Valentina stood up, feeling a little shaky and disbelieving. She'd imagined Gio telling her she could work on the lowest rung of the ladder in his kitchen. Not that she could be handed the entire catering job for the Corretti Cup! Suspicious now she said testily, 'I'm not a charity case.'

His eyes flashed and his jaw tightened. 'I don't hire people out of the goodness of my heart. I hire them because they're good. I've got a new chef that I'm not sure about so I want you to devise a menu for him to work to. I saw what you did at the wedding reception—your work is good, very good. Quite apart from the recommendation that my aunt hired you in the first place when she's a notorious stickler for perfection.'

A warm flush of pleasure took Valentina by surprise and she realised what an opportunity she was being presented with. The annual Corretti Cup was a very prestigious international fixture. Whatever the kudos of doing a Corretti wedding, this was on another level. Suddenly she felt giddy at the thought.

She bit her lip. 'I had two full-time staff working for me. I trust them.'

Gio waved a hand. 'Hire them back. Whatever you need.'

He came back around his desk and sat down and looked up at her, completely business-like. 'Let's discuss your fees.'

An hour later Valentina's head was whirling. She'd been despatched with one of Gio's assistants and given a thorough tour of the kitchens and dining areas. It was all state of the art and luxurious without being ostentatious. There were VIP corporate boxes that overlooked the stadium, with their own balconies. There was even a couple of royal suite boxes.

When they emerged back out onto the main track area her guide pointed behind the huge stand and said, 'That's where the stables and practice gallops are situated, and the staff living quarters. Signor Corretti keeps the rest of his horses at his *castello* nearby where his stud is based.'

Valentina pushed down the lancing pain when she thought of the *castello* grounds where Mario had died and asked, 'What's it like to work here?'

The assistant answered enthusiastically, 'Signor Corretti is a tough boss but fair. He always knows exactly what's going on, and we get better paid than at any of the other racetracks in Italy.'

Valentina told him she was fine to wander on her own after that. The truth was, Gio had been more than fair with her pay. He'd been positively generous. When she'd balked at the amount, he'd said, 'I pay all my staff well, Valentina. I'm not interested in having people working for me who are grumbling about pay or overtime. I can do this, and so I do.'

Valentina surmised now that the vast wealth he'd built up from his horses came in handy when you wanted to keep your employees loyal. But for some reason that churlish thought didn't sit entirely right. Gio hadn't struck her as the type of person to buy his staff's favour. They all seemed to genuinely like him.

She saw his tall form now in the distance and it made her heart kick in a very betraying manner. He'd spotted her and was striding towards her. Valentina had the abrupt urge to turn and run away fast but she didn't. When he stopped before her he asked her how she'd got on and she told him. Dark glasses hid his eyes and Valentina had the perverse urge to take them off so she could read those changeable green depths.

She curled her hands to fists at her sides.

'So you'll start tomorrow then? There's a lot to do in three weeks.'

Valentina nodded and looked away. 'Yes, I'll start tomorrow.' She looked back to Gio and said haltingly, 'I… just wanted to say thank you. You didn't have to do this.'

Mario. Of course he had to do this.

The name hung in the air between them again, even though neither of them had said it. Gio shrugged lightly.

'I'm always on the lookout for good staff and I think you'll add an edge to this year's Corretti Cup.'

He was perfectly solicitous and polite, much as Valentina would imagine him being with anyone else, and she suddenly hated that. She didn't want to be just another employee. So what did she want to be then? The dangerous revelation of that thought made her step back hurriedly. 'OK, well, I'd better get going.'

'You know you can move into the staff quarters here if you like?'

Valentina shook her head. 'No, with my father in hospital I'd like to see him every day. And my mother needs me.'

'That's going to be a killer of a commute. I don't need you falling asleep in your canapés.'

Valentina glanced quickly at him and away again when she saw his rigid jaw. 'It'll be fine. I won't let you down.'

She moved to leave and Gio put his hand on her arm. She stopped in her tracks, breathless.

'I didn't mean that you would let me down. I'm concerned it'll be too much.'

Valentina forced down the tender feeling rising up and looked directly at Gio's dark glasses where she was reflected as a tiny figure. She pulled her arm free and said coolly, 'I'm not your concern.'

Gio's jaw clenched tighter. 'You are if you're my employee.'

Valentina faced him directly, something dark goading her to say, 'Since when have you cared so much for others or their safety?'

Gio seemed to blanch before her eyes and Valentina wished the words unsaid but it was too late. She stepped back before she said anything else. 'You don't need to worry.'

Gio watched Valentina hurry away in her black slacks

and white shirt with her hair pulled back and he wanted to throttle her. Well, he wanted to kiss her, and then throttle her. He was glad of his glasses because he'd been staring at her mouth for the past few minutes, until she'd let that little barb slide out: *Since when have you cared so much for others...*

Gio swung away abruptly from following Valentina's progress to the car park and paced angrily towards his own jeep which was nearby. He gunned the engine and made the fifteen-minute journey to his *castello* with his hands clenched tight around the wheel.

When he saw the familiar lines and ramparts of his home he breathed out and turned into the impressive drive-way lined by tall cypress trees. As the *castello* came into view he had to concede as he often did that it was entirely too huge for just him, but he'd bought it more for the surrounding land which contained his small farm and more importantly his stud and stables.

It had used to also contain a small training ground and gallops but after Mario's death he'd got rid of them, unable to look out his window and not see the prone figure of his best friend lying on the ground.

It was one of the reasons he'd taken off for Europe after Mario's death and had spent the best part of two years in a blurry haze. Anything to avoid coming home and dealing with his demons. But he had eventually found his way back out of that black hole to come home. Now, he still trained horses but he was fanatical about safety and hadn't been on a horse's back in seven years.

Cursing this uncharacteristic introspection Gio swung out of his jeep and instead of going into the house, took a detour around it and made directly for the stables where he found Misfit, who whinnied in acknowledgement as soon as Gio drew near. Just being near his prize stallion made a level of peace flow through Gio, even though having met Valentina again he realised peace was bound to be elusive.

He caressed the sleek thoroughbred's neck and face and chuckled softly before taking an apple out of his pocket, which the horse gratefully received. 'You're a rogue,' Gio chastised easily. 'You only love me for my apples.' Familiar emotion welled up when he thought of how far he'd come with this thoroughbred.

His father, who had fancied himself as a bit of a horse-man on the side, had installed state-of-the-art stables and training grounds at the family palazzo. It had quickly become a sanctuary for Gio, who'd had an innate affinity for the horses from the first moment he'd seen one.

Benito Corretti had bought Misfit as a yearling, unbroken, from a stud in Ireland. The colt had had a good pedigree but after several failed attempts to break him in by the head trainer, his father had declared curtly, 'Send him to the meat factory. He was a waste of money.'

Gio had gone to his father. He'd been sixteen years old and hadn't stuttered in a couple of years but in front of his father he could feel his vocal chords closing up the way they always had, but he'd swallowed hard and concentrated. 'Father, give me a week—if I can't break him by then you can do what you want.'

His father had been drunk and had taunted Gio cruelly, 'Are you s-s-s-s-sure, G-G-G-Gio?'

His father couldn't resist the chance to goad him. Gio wanted to punch him in the face but held his fists by his side. How many times had Mario counselled him that it wasn't worth it to show emotion to his old man? As soon as he could he'd be gone from his family palazzo to set up his own business. Somewhere far, far away.

His opportunity to do just that had come much sooner than he'd thought. Gio had confounded everyone by tam-

ing the horse within a week and his father had said grudgingly, 'You can have him then, seeing as how you put so
much work into him—perhaps you're not a complete loss
to the Corretti name after all.'

Gio had seized his opportunity. He'd never excelled at
school anyway, so he'd left his house that night and with
the help of Mario had taken his horse to a stables nearby. In
the following weeks Gio had searched for and found work
at another stables near Syracuse, and had made a deal with
the owner so that he could work for food and board while
stabling his horse there for free. He'd trained his horse in
his free time, honing him into a champion.

His boss had seen something in Gio and the horse—
when he'd been transporting his own horses to race in
England, Ireland and France, he'd offered to include Gio's
horse, Misfit. Gio had never looked back after that. Misfit had become a champion racer almost overnight and
Gio had paid back his mentor and boss many times over.

He'd been winning millions at the biggest racetracks in
Europe by the time he was nineteen, making a name for
himself as a prodigiously natural trainer and then breeder.

Misfit had been retired for a long time now, but with
his stellar track record, horse breeders from as far away
as the Middle East and Ireland sent their mares to Sicily
to be covered by the renowned stallion for astronomical
fees. He'd already sired at least another dozen champions.

Gio ran a cursory but expert eye over his horse now and,
satisfied that he was in good condition and comfortable,
gave him a last affectionate pat on the neck. As he was
walking back out of the stables all he could think about
though was how the hell he was going to get through the
foreseeable future with Valentina Ferranti around every
corner....

* * *

By the end of the first week Valentina could hardly see
straight she was so tired. She was driving almost two hours
each way every day in her clapped-out car and after calling
in to see her father in hospital it was usually after midnight
before she got to bed, before getting up again at 5:00 a.m.

Her father's condition was not good. He was on a waiting list for a major heart operation but it could take months
for him to be next in line. The very real fear that he could
have another heart attack, and this time a worse one before
the operation, was constantly on Valentina's mind. Not to
mention her mother, who was beside herself with worry.

She was in the act of turning with a plate of pastries in
her hands when the door to the kitchen opened, startling
her. When Valentina saw who it was, the plate slipped out
of her fingers, smashing all over the floor.

Even the sound couldn't really jar her out of her exhaus-
tion as she bent to start picking up the pieces.

'Wait, let me do that.'

Valentina stood reluctantly and watched as Gio bent
down at her feet and started picking up the biggest pieces.
One of the evening cleaners came in then and Gio instructed him to clean up the mess. He took Valentina by
the arm and led her out, protesting, 'I should clean it up—
it's my mess.'

'Leave it,' growled Gio before letting her arm go and
turning to face her outside the kitchen door. Nearly everyone else had already left for the evening.

Gio looked at his watch and asked, 'What on earth are
you doing here at 8:30 p.m.?'

Valentina flushed, far too aware of Gio's earthy smell—
musky and masculine. He must have been working with
the horses. He seemed very tall and imposing right then,
his broad shoulders blocking everything out behind him,

making a curious ache form in Valentina's belly. She hadn't seen him much during the week and she only realised now as some tension ebbed away that she'd been unconsciously *waiting* for him. It made her angry and she glared up at him, hands on hips. 'I'm working late because it's the only quiet time in the kitchen when I can experiment with new recipes.'

'Working late isn't a problem, as long as you start work late, but you've been in every morning this week at 7:00 a.m., well before most other people.'

'How do you know?' Valentina asked suspiciously.

'Because it's my business to know these things.'

Valentina bit her lip when she could feel a retort springing up. She remembered the last time and how her cruel words had rang in her head for days afterwards.

'Fine,' she said grudgingly, 'I won't work so late from now on.'

Gio sounded grim. 'You look exhausted, and I don't believe you.'

Valentina looked up at him and was actually too tired at that moment to argue. All she could do was wearily pull her apron over her head and say, 'Well, then you won't stop me going home.'

Gio took her arm and all but frog-marched her out to where his jeep was waiting. 'I'm driving you—you're a liability.'

Valentina started to protest but he all but lifted her into the passenger seat and secured the seat belt around her. Her mouth was open to say something but when the hard muscles of his arm brushed her breast she shut it abruptly, heat flashing up through her body.

As grim-faced as Gio, Valentina crossed her arms and once they were on the main road to Palermo she managed to get out a strangled, 'How am I supposed to get to work in the morning or are you providing a personal chauffeur service to your staff now?'

Gio sent her a quelling look. 'It's Saturday tomorrow so you shouldn't be working anyway, but I'll have someone drop your car home for you.'

When they were reaching the outskirts of Palermo, in about half the time it would have taken Valentina, she said, 'I need to stop at the hospital first.'

Gio obliged and took the road to the hospital and when he got out of the jeep and met her at the front she stopped and said, 'What are you doing? I can get a taxi home from here.'

'I'd like to pay my respects to your mother if I may, and your father if he doesn't mind.'

Valentina couldn't speak. Guilt flooded her and she avoided Gio's eyes. Under his questioning look she blurted out, 'The truth is that my parents don't know about...my job. That I lost it, or that I'm working for you.'

Gio folded his arms; his belly felt leaden. 'And you think they'd be upset if they knew?'

She looked up at him. 'Well, what do you think?'

A bleak feeling rushed through Gio. How could he have forgotten for a moment the intense and awful grief of that day by the graveside. He ran a hand through his hair and stepped back. 'You're probably right...it's not a good idea.'

'What's not a good idea? Gio, I'm glad you came— Emilio has been asking for you.'

They both turned at the same time to see Valentina's mother on the steps of the hospital where she'd clearly been getting air and had heard their last exchange. With no choice now, Gio followed a stony-faced Valentina and her mother into the hospital, his stomach churning at the thought of what lay ahead.

CHAPTER FOUR

'WHAT DID YOU say to my father?' Valentina hissed at Gio as they walked back out of the hospital an hour later.

Gio was still in shock himself at how Emilio had re-acted to seeing him. Alone in the hospital room with the old man, Gio had steeled himself for whatever Mario's father was going to say, expecting a diatribe or a level of hostility matched by his daughter. But the man had completely taken the wind out of his sails by saying a little stiffly, 'First of all, thank you. I believe the reason I'm still alive is because of you.'

Gio had muttered something unintelligible, embarrassed.

And then Signor Ferranti had held out his hand. 'Come here, boy...let me look at you.'

Gio had walked over and given his hand to Emilio, who had taken it in a surprisingly strong grip. His voice was rougher, emotional. 'When we lost Mario...we lost you too.'

Gio's mouth had opened and closed. His own emotion rising thick and fast. Eventually he'd got out, 'But...don't you blame me? Hate me for what happened?'

Emilio had let his hand go and pointed to a chair for Gio to sit down and he'd done so, heavily. Stunned.

'I did,' the old man admitted, 'for a long time. It was

easier to blame you than to believe that it could have just been a tragic accident. But ultimately, that's what it was. I know well how reckless Mario was, you were as bad as each other.'

'If I hadn't had that cursed horse though—'

Signor Ferranti put up a hand, stopping Gio. He arched a brow. 'Do you really think you could have stopped Mario when he wanted to do something?'

Gio's chest was so tight he could hardly breathe. He half shrugged.

Mario's father said gently now, 'Mario followed you around like a puppy, wanted to do everything you did....'

A granite weight settled in Gio's belly, the all-too-familiar guilt rearing up when he thought of the countless reckless activities he'd encouraged Mario to join him in over the years. Anything to alleviate his own sense of yawning loneliness. 'I know,' he'd just answered quietly.

As if sensing his self-flagellation though, Valentina's father had said gently, 'Gio, he worshipped the ground you walked on...just as I know you did him.'

Gio looked at Signor Ferranti in surprise. There was no condemnation in his voice, only weary acceptance.

'For Valentina though...it was very hard for her to come to terms with. She was so angry...is still angry, I think.'

'Gio!'

Gio looked down at Valentina blankly for a second. He was still in the room with her father. They were outside the hospital doors now and her arms were folded and she was glaring up at him. There were smudges of weariness under her eyes and that made Gio's resolve firm even more.

Now she'd got his attention she continued. 'So are you going to tell me how on earth you had the nerve to propose moving my father to a private specialist clinic in Syracuse, let alone taking him to a hospital on the mainland for a major heart operation?'

Gio reigned in his temper which seemed to be growing a shorter and shorter fuse around this woman. He took a deep breath. 'I offered to help your father and I'm glad to say he accepted. By moving him to Syracuse while he waits for the operation, you will be able to move into the staff accommodation at the racetrack. It'll wipe out your commute and give you an easy mind with your parents so close. It'll also ease their minds to know you're not over-exhausting yourself.'

'So you're doing this to make things better for yourself?' Valentina sneered. 'Because you don't want a fainting staff member serving your VIP guests?'

Valentina wasn't sure why she was so angry, just that she was. Blistering. It was something to do with the way her father had shown no enmity towards Gio. And it was more than just gratitude for having saved his life. After a long private conversation, she and her mother had been allowed back into the room and the first thing her father had said to her was, 'You should have told us about your job, *piccolina.…*'

So not only had Gio told them about her disaster, they also now knew that she was working for him. And didn't seem fazed by that knowledge at all. She'd looked at Gio accusingly but his face had been completely impassive.

If anything, her parents had been looking at Gio almost adoringly. And then her father's consultant had come into the room and Gio had cleared his throat and announced what he would like to do to help.

Her parents had been taken aback by his audacious offer and Valentina had looked on in shock as her mother had gripped her husband's hand and begged him with tears in her eyes to do as Gio suggested.

'What's the problem, Valentina? I would have thought you'd be happy to know that your father will be receiving the best treatment.'

Valentina uncrossed her arms and her hands curled to fists by her sides. 'You put them, *all of us*, in an awkward position—how could they say no? But you know we can't afford this treatment. How do you think we can ever pay you back?'

Gio's face tightened. He waved a hand. 'You don't need to worry about that. I'll take care of it.'

He started to walk towards his jeep and Valentina called impetuously from behind him, 'Do you really think money will make up for it?'

Gio stopped in his tracks and after long silent tense seconds he turned around from the bottom of the steps. His face was stark. 'What's that supposed to mean?'

Valentina had gone too far now. Something very personal and dark was pushing her over this edge. 'You know what I'm talking about. You're trying to atone—'

Gio bounded up the steps again so fast and with such ruthless intent that Valentina took a step back.

'So what if I am?' he asked rawly. 'Is that so bad if it saves your father?'

Valentina felt like something was breaking apart inside her. 'Yes. Because it won't bring *him* back.'

Gio took her arms in a tight grip with his hands. 'Do you think I don't know that?'

For a second Valentina glimpsed a depth and level of stark pain in Gio's eyes that made her want to cry out. It echoed within her like a keening cry. And another echo sounded deep within her, telling her she was a fraud of the worst kind, because she was deliberately pushing Gio away to avoid facing up to a dark truth inside her.

It was the same reason she'd hurled those cruel words

at him last week at the track: *Since when have you cared so much for others...*

She'd been able to push it down for seven years, but standing in front of him now—it was rising inexorably within her, demanding that she acknowledge it. And she couldn't. Gio was unwittingly forcing her look at herself and she didn't like what she saw. Breaking the intense eye contact Valentina ripped herself free of his grip and stepped around him to hurry down the steps. She went straight to a nearby hospital taxi rank.

Before Gio could stop her she'd got into the first taxi and was pulling out of the hospital forecourt. He looked at the taxi's break lights winking just before it disappeared completely. A wave of bleakness washed over him. Was Valentina right? Was he interfering where he shouldn't? Acting out of a crippling sense of guilt? Trying to buy his soul back by saving Mario's father?

The fact that Mario's parents had apparently forgiven Gio was small comfort now. Gio knew that the only hope he had for his soul to find some peace was through Valentina's forgiveness, and her father's words came back to Gio then: *It was very hard for her to come to terms with... she was so angry...she still is.*

The anger Valentina felt was palpable, not in question. She'd only come to him for help because he was literally the only person on the island who would defy his aunt to employ her. His mouth firmed and he made his way to his jeep. He would not apologise for wanting to help her father and he was *not* doing it to buy forgiveness. He was doing it because Mario wasn't here to take care of his family, but Gio was. And Valentina could rant and rail all she liked.

Valentina stared blindly out of the taxi window, the lights of a busy Friday Palermo night flashing past. But the lights blurred as weak ineffectual tears filled her eyes. She'd just run away like the abject coward that she was. Angry with herself for feeling so emotional, Valentina dashed them away, avoiding the driver's curious glances in the rearview mirror.

She hated the ease with which Gio had been so comprehensively all but welcomed back into the bosom of her family. She hated the ease with which he was able to guarantee her father's well-being. And she hated *herself* for being like this.

Gio was highlighting the big flaw that was Valentina in her own family. Mario had been the one on whom all hopes and dreams had rested. So Valentina had been more or less forgotten about. Not the most academic of students anyway, she'd left school at sixteen to work with her grandmother in the small trattoria.

Mario had known of her ambitions to succeed and make something of herself. But when he'd died, that link had gone and her parents had been despondent, left with their only other child who had no glittering prospects.

That's why Valentina had worked so hard to build up a business. But even when it had taken off, her parents had been wary more than proud. They were of the old school and thought that what really counted was academic qualification and a solid career. And also that Valentina should find a nice man and settle down, find someone who would provide for her…and them. Provide them with grandchildren.

But instead, her nemesis Giacomo Corretti had been the one to step into the breach. In more ways than one. Little by little she was becoming more and more beholden to him. She resented him for it but then she'd been the one to invite him back into their lives so she had no one to blame but herself.

She remembered what it had been like to look into his eyes just now, to see the abject pain in those green and brown depths. The way her heart had clenched, the way her conscience had mocked her. And worse, the way her pulse had pounded with a deeply unsettling rhythm just to be near him. As it always did, as it always *had*. Why did he still have to have this effect on her?

The taxi was pulling up outside her apartment building now and Valentina paid the driver and refused to let Gio dominate her thoughts any more. It was only when she fell into a fitful sleep sometime later that he came to haunt her in her dreams.

'What's this?'

Valentina stood in front of Gio the following Monday morning in his office. Her head was still reeling at how fast things had moved in just thirty-six hours. Her father was already settled in the private clinic in Syracuse and she'd moved into the staff accommodation the previous evening.

Gio was sitting behind his desk looking absurdly out of place in his grey T-shirt. He looked far too vital and virile and *sexy* to be sitting at a desk.

Valentina dragged her attention back to his question. 'It's the advance on my pay that you gave me. I need to pay you back for what you're doing for my father. I realise that it'll take a lot—'

Gio stood up abruptly, making Valentina stop talking. His face had darkened visibly and he held the cheque back out to her. 'Don't insult me, Valentina. Please.'

Valentina refused to take the cheque, her own face darkening as blood rushed into it. She felt embarrassed. 'When I came to you looking for work it was to make enough money to support and care for my parents. What I earn should go into their care and as you're paying for that at the moment…' She trailed off, a little scared at the way Gio's eyes had darkened almost to black by now.

'I offered to pay for your father's treatment with no strings attached.'

Valentina observed scathingly, 'There's always strings attached.'

Gio shook his head and looked at her pityingly, making a hot rush of humiliation rush through Valentina. He came around his desk to face her and she wished he hadn't. In flat runners he towered over her own not inconsiderable five feet seven inches.

'What happened to you? What made you become so cynical?' He frowned. 'Was it a love affair gone wrong?'

Valentina nearly choked. A love affair gone wrong? Gio had no idea. She'd had plenty of men chasing after her but she'd kept them all at arm's length. Terrified on some level of getting close to anyone. Terrified of the way one minute someone you loved could be there, and the next minute they could be *gone*. For ever. That realisation seemed to explode into her consciousness like a bomb going off. She'd never even really articulated it to herself like that before. She'd just always instinctively avoided relationships. Losing Mario had made her cynical. It had twisted something inside her soul.

Made weak by this insight, Valentina was barely aware when Gio took her hand and folded the cheque back into it, closing her fingers over it. His hand was big and warm around hers and she looked up at him. They were standing much closer than she'd realised and his scent, musky and warm, unleashed an avalanche of vivid memories in her imagination.

Jerkily she pulled her hand back from his, with the cheque in it, and stepped back. The only coherent thing in her head was that she needed to get out of there *now*.

Before Gio saw something she herself couldn't really understand.

She got to the door and then looked back and blurted out, 'It was you. You made me like this.'

All Valentina saw before she fled was Gio's face darkening even more. She made her way back to the kitchen and busied herself, silently begging everyone around her to leave her alone.

Where did she get the nerve to say these things to him? It was as if every time he came within feet of her she had to lash out. Say the worst thing possible, terrified that if he got too close he might see her cruel words for what they were—a very flimsy attempt to keep him at a distance at all costs.

Valentina knew on some rational level that Mario's death had been a tragic accident; Gio hadn't forced her brother onto that demonic horse. She'd even heard him discouraging it, *initially*. The knowledge that her parents appeared able to forgive him had been a huge blow to her own justification to stay angry at him. But the fact was, for so long now she'd held Gio responsible.

Her anger had been compounded by the way he'd disappeared after Mario's death only to turn up playing the part of a playboy bent on nothing but slaking his basest needs. Disgusted with herself for having been so invested in what he was doing, Valentina had nevertheless stored up every tiny example of Gio carousing and generally acting as if he didn't have a care in the world, while they'd mourned Mario.

Her anger at him had always comforted her on some level. It was familiar and…necessary. For her sanity. In all honesty Valentina knew that she was very afraid of looking at what might be left behind if she couldn't hold Gio responsible. If she couldn't be angry with him. That thought was so terrifying that something must have shown on her face.

'Val? Are you OK?'

Valentina sucked in a big breath and forced a smile at Franco, who was looking at her intently across the island they were working at. She nodded abruptly. 'Fine…I, ah, just remembered something I need to do.'

Thankfully he left her alone and that evening Valentina escaped to the clinic to see how her parents were settling in, rather than unpack in her new accommodation, telling herself it was more than just a ruse to avoid bumping into Gio again.

That evening Gio cursed volubly outside Valentina's suite of rooms. There was no answer. She wasn't there. Even though he knew logically she was most likely visiting her parents, he had to battle a spiking of something very proprietorial. And he didn't like it.

Women had never been anything more than a diversion to him. His long childhood years of feeling less than, and inadequate, had left him with too many scars to trust anyone, apart from Mario. His subsequent successes had done much to chase away that sense of inadequacy, but since Mario's death, the joy had been taken out of it to a large extent.

Gio's mouth twisted wryly just remembering how Mario had been the one who'd fallen in and out of love like some besotted Romeo. Something within Gio had always remained aloof with a woman. They hadn't ever touched some deep secret part of him. In the two years after Mario's death there had been an endless parade of beautiful women but none he'd connected with, and more often than not Gio had found himself waking alone.

Valentina. She'd always been different. She'd snuck into

a place that was locked away deep inside him. But he'd been acutely aware that his feelings and desires for her were strictly forbidden.

When he'd left Sicily first she'd been only ten or eleven. A gap-toothed child only on his radar as his best friend's kid sister who had trailed them with almost religious devotion.

But when he'd returned years later—a millionaire, the new owner of the racetrack in Syracuse with plans to rebuild—she'd been fifteen. And Gio had found himself aware of her in a way that had made him ashamed. So he'd flung himself into socialising with Mario, pursuing the local beauties, anything to push dangerous thoughts and desires from his mind.

Over the next two years she'd only grown more and more beautiful and mature. She'd started to flirt with him, but with such sweet innocence that it had twisted his heart. One day he'd been weak. She'd arrived to look for Mario, who'd already left. A miscommunication. Gio had seen her get startled by Misfit and had acted on an impulse, lifting her onto the horse.

He'd swung up behind her, wrapping his arm around her taut young body. The weight of her firm breasts had been heavy on his arm. Those stolen indulgent minutes had been the most erotic in his life.…

Gio grimaced now and turned away from Valentina's door. What was he doing hanging around like some besotted fool? Yes, he still wanted her. More than ever. But that was all. The capacity to feel anything more had long ago withered to dust inside him, poisoned by grief and guilt.

And Valentina…? She hated him with every cell in her body and if she *had* ever felt anything for him, physical or otherwise, it had been destroyed that night in the hospital in Palermo when she'd seen her dead brother laid out on a slab in the morgue.

* * *

The Corretti Cup was fast approaching. Valentina and her staff were flat-out making sure they had everything ordered and organised. That evening as she hung up her apron, she had to concede reluctantly that Gio had done her a favour by insisting she stay on-site. She wasn't half as exhausted as she had been. And the lines of worry and stress had disappeared from her parents' faces.

She'd avoided him since their last cataclysmic meeting the day before and she didn't like the way guilt pricked her conscience *again*. Driving down that disturbing feeling, Valentina walked around the front of the stadium to get back to her accommodation.

She had a suite of rooms to herself, complete with a kitchenette, living area and en suite bedroom. The understated opulence of the accommodation had blown her away. It was in an old reconverted stone stables. She had a private balcony which looked out over the back of the stadium where the gallops, stables and training ground was based.

But she loved this view over the racetrack. The sun was setting over the sea in the distance, turning everything golden and orange. She stood at the railing and sighed deeply, and then heard from not far away, 'It's beautiful when it's like this, with no one around. That'll all change in a few days though.'

Valentina had tensed at the first word. She turned her head and saw Gio sitting on one of the stand seats behind her—that's how she'd missed him. The thought of him watching her for those few seconds made her feel warm. Instantly she doused it. 'Yes,' she said stiffly, 'it's lovely.'

She made to walk on but Gio lifted something out of an ice bucket beside him and she realised he was holding out a beer, and that he had his own one in his other hand.

Ice cold water droplets ran down the side of the cold bottle and suddenly she was parched.

She looked at Gio and all she could see were those broad shoulders and his messy hair, flopping over one eye. She felt weak. He said easily, 'I bring out some beers for the racetrack workers most evenings. It's a tough few weeks getting ready for the cup.'

Torn between wanting to run and wanting to stay, which was very disturbing, Valentina remembered what she'd said the previous day and then stepped forward and took the bottle. Her fingers brushed off Gio's, sending a spark of awareness jumping between them. 'Thanks.'

She stepped over the bottom seat and sat down near him, and then looked at the view again as if it was the most absorbing thing she'd ever seen. She took a gulp of cold beer, not really tasting it. Silence grew and lengthened between them and she fiddled with the label on her bottle. Unable to stand it any more she turned to face him. Awkwardly she started, 'I…I've said things to you…'

She stopped, cursing her inability to be articulate and tried again. 'I owe you an apology. What I said yesterday…' She shrugged one shoulder minutely. 'You seem to bring out the worst in me.'

Gio shook his head, his eyes unreadable in the growing gloom. 'Valentina, what happened in the past—'

She cut him off with an urgent appeal, suddenly terrified he'd mention Mario. 'Let's not talk about it, OK?'

Gio closed his mouth. She could see his jaw clench, but then he just said, 'OK, fine.'

Valentina turned back to the view, an altogether edgier tension in the air now. Desperate to find something, anything innocuous, to talk about she seized on something she'd overheard earlier. 'Some of the staff were talking about the regeneration project for the docklands. It sounds interesting.'

Gio looked at Valentina's profile. The straight nose, determined chin. Long dark lashes. The graceful curve of her cheekbone. She was trying to make small talk. The moment felt very fragile, a tentative cessation of hostilities. Gio's mouth tightened. 'It's a project put in place primarily by my grandfather, Salvatore, in some kind of effort to bring everyone together. Hence the grand wedding that never happened.'

Valentina looked at Gio. 'Isn't that a good thing—I mean, not the wedding failing but bringing everyone together?'

He smiled tightly. 'It would be if everyone's interests were altruistic.'

Valentina frowned. 'Are your interests different to the others?'

Gio shifted; they were straying into an area he wasn't entirely comfortable with now. Reluctantly he said, 'I've been interested in the docklands area for some time. I think it could be a very useful space for youth projects.'

'What kind of youth projects?'

Gio shrugged, tense. 'The kind of projects that brings kids together, teaches them things, lets them explore their limits in a safe environment. Gets them off the streets basically.'

Brings them together so they don't feel so isolated, like I always did even with Mario...

Gio clamped his jaw shut as if those rogue words might spill out. He wasn't sure why he felt so vulnerable telling her about something that was so close to his heart. Was he afraid she'd laugh at him? Accuse him again of trying to atone?

Valentina seemed to absorb this information in silence

and then she asked, 'Your brothers were mentioned too. Do you see them much?'

Gio's mouth tightened. Little did she realise that any question about his family was akin to walking blindfolded into a minefield. He dragged his gaze away from the provocative curves of her body beside him in simple jeans and T-shirt and looked out to the falling night. 'No…is the simple answer.'

'They weren't at the wedding?'

Gio shrugged. 'Not that I saw. They should have been.' He took a gulp of beer, suddenly wondering if he'd been wise to alert Valentina to his presence here.

He felt her turn to look at him. 'You didn't spend much time with them growing up, did you?'

He glanced at her then and took another gulp of beer and swallowed. 'You know I didn't.' Because he spent all his time with Mario. He didn't have to say it.

'Were they mean to you?'

Gio looked away again. *What was this? Twenty questions?* But he unclenched his jaw. 'No, they were never mean to me. They had their own battles to fight. They both took more after my father than I did. I never had that drive or ambition, that sense of competition to be the dominant Corretti. They just…they were preoccupied with their own stuff.'

Gio glanced at Valentina again and she was looking down into her beer bottle, swirling the liquid. Her hands were small and graceful. Capable. He had a sudden memory of being much smaller, when Valentina had been sitting on the sidelines of some game he and Mario had been playing.

At one point he'd gone up to her and asked if she wanted to join in, stuttering over the words. Instinctively he'd been tensed for her reaction, to laugh at him or mimic him, but she'd just stood up and put her hand in his.

Sounding as if it was almost half to herself Valentina said now, 'You've been very successful.'

Gio smiled minutely, brought back to the present, and the reality of a very adult Valentina. 'The horse-racing business is very lucrative and I had a good horse.'

Valentina smiled wryly. That was an understatement. Everyone knew about Giacomo Corretti's meteoric rise to fame and the horse that had won races for almost a decade, turning him from champion into legend. She looked at him. 'Is Misfit still alive?'

Gio nodded and something about the intensity of his focus on her made her nervous, tingly.

'Yes…but he's retired now. He stands at my stud at the *castello*. Mares are sent from all over the world to be covered by him. He's sired two of my current champions— Mischief and Misdemeanour. They're both running in the Corretti Cup this year.'

Valentina fell silent. Misfit had been the horse that he'd taken her riding on that day around the gallops. The sheer provocation of that memory again, and the way this conversation had veered wildly off a comfortable track, made her put her beer bottle down and she stood up.

She sounded breathless. 'I should be going.'

Gio stood up too, and it was only then that Valentina realised how dark it had become. His face was shadowed. He looked even bigger in the dim light. It was as if thinking of that moment on the horse had ripped away some vital part of her defence around this man. She felt naked, vulnerable. Exposed.

She turned around and then felt a large warm hand on her arm, under her T-shirt. Her belly plummeted to some dark hot place.

Gio compelled her to face him, turning her around. He was frowning. 'What did I say?'

'No—nothing,' Valentina stuttered, which made her think of Gio's stutter. How fierce and yet vulnerable he'd looked whenever he had stuttered. She closed her eyes. *Dio.* Would her imagination not cease?

'I've upset you.'

Valentina opened her eyes but avoided his, focusing on the bronzed column of his throat above his dark T-shirt. She shook her head. 'No…I'm just tired. It's been a long day…few days.'

'Valentina, look at me.'

Somehow Gio was right in front of her, his hand hot on her arm. She imagined that she could feel her pulse beating against her skin, as if trying to touch his skin. His blood.

She looked up and was caught by his dark brown gaze. Green flecks like dark jewels. How many times had she dreamt of these eyes? How many times had she coveted his gaze on her, only to feel it and flee like a little coward? His gaze was on her now and it was scorching her alive.

Gio frowned even more, in a question. 'Valentina?'

Her eyes dropped to Gio's mouth. That gorgeous sensual mouth. Made for dark things. When she'd been seventeen she'd kissed her pillow and imagined she was kissing him.

Gio's voice sounded slightly rough. 'Why are you looking at me like that?'

Her eyes rose to meet his. She seemed to have been invaded by some kind of lethargy. She knew she should be cool, step back, push his arm off her, but all those things seemed so difficult to do.

She shook her head faintly. 'Looking at you…like what?'

A long moment burned between them. Valentina had forgotten everything. She could feel herself swaying ever so slightly towards Gio. And then his other hand came onto her other arm and he was pushing her back, pushing her *away* from him.

It was as if someone had just doused her in cold water. Valentina suddenly saw exactly what she must have looked like. Staring at Gio's mouth like a love-struck teenager, swaying like a drunk person, silently begging him— She stepped back sharply, forcing his hands to drop. She felt hot inside, her skin prickly all over, and worse, her breasts felt fuller, her nipples stinging against the lace of her bra.

'Go to bed, Valentina, you're tired.' Gio's voice was curt and flayed Valentina alive.

She couldn't even answer. She stepped down from the seats and had to force herself not to run all the way to her rooms. Mortification was a tidal wave eating her up all over. Gio had pushed her back; he'd had to stop her from making a complete fool of herself. She'd just exposed herself to him spectacularly. No matter what she said or did from now on, she hadn't hidden her attraction to him.

Surrounded by the inky blackness of the night, Gio downed the rest of his beer in a disgusted gulp. When he'd stood in front of Valentina…and she'd looked at him. *Cristo.* He'd been so hot and hungry for her that he'd imagined her looking at him as if…as if she wanted to kiss him, or for him to kiss her.

He'd been so close to pulling her into him, tipping up that chin, running a thumb across the silky skin of her jaw and cheek.… He's almost done it, and then he'd seen her sway slightly…*with fatigue, not lust.*

Thank God he hadn't completely lost it and misread her signals. The last thing he needed was to add one more thing to Valentina's hate list for him.

CHAPTER FIVE

THE FOLLOWING EVENING Valentina was in foul form. It had been a tough day; everyone's nerves were on edge as they put together all the elements for the Corretti Cup. There were many more staff now, all labouring in their various departments. Event micro-managers were making sure all the areas were kitted out. There was one central dining area where a set menu buffet lunch would be served every day for the main crowd.

Then there was the unbelievably opulent cordoned-off vast VIP marquee area, set in its own landscaped gardens, which had the sit-down à la carte menu, and where each evening a champagne reception would be held as the last races were run.

On the last night there would be a gala ball which would include a charity auction. All the staff had been kitted out with security passes for various areas. Valentina had received one for all areas. She was supervising both the main and VIP areas and Gio was adamant that the buffet diners shouldn't feel like they were getting a second-rate service.

It had surprised her; she'd expected him to be more concerned with the VIP section but he'd been almost disdainful of that as he'd led the group of his chief organisers around that morning, making last-minute notes. Some people were paying into the thousands for tickets into the

VIP marquee, or for a corporate box at the stadium stand. Valentina had also been surprised to learn via one of the other staff that all of the proceeds of the Corretti Cup VIP ticket sales were going to various charities Gio supported locally.

On top of all of that she knew he was dealing with the arrival of hundreds of horses for the races. Some of the most expensive and valuable bloodstock in the world was now at the Corretti stables along with an accompanying heavy security presence. The place was buzzing with grooms and cleaners and decorators and assistants.

Gio had been nothing but utterly professional to her all day, and distant—he'd barely looked at her that morning during the walkabout meeting. He'd treated her exactly the same as the others, who'd all been feverishly taking notes. She should be happy; she should be delighted that the previous evening appeared not to have had any effect on his behaviour towards her. She should be ecstatic he was practically ignoring her!

So why was she so out of sorts? She was two days away from the most important opportunity of her career and she couldn't afford to mess up or get distracted.

Thoroughly disgruntled, Valentina went to see her parents after work and brought them some food she'd prepared. They wanted to hear all about the lavish preparations at the racetrack as it was all anyone could talk about in Syracuse. It was the biggest annual event attracting thousands of tourists. It shamed her a little to realise just how much Gio was doing for the local economy.

When she was walking out about thirty minutes later, her mother stopped Valentina in the corridor. 'Gio came to see us yesterday. He's been very good, making sure everything is on track for the operation.'

Valentina's voice was instantly tight. 'Did he? That's

nice.' Another surprise—in the midst of his busiest time of the year he was taking time to visit her parents?

Her mother shook her head, her dark eyes compassionate. 'Valentina…he has suffered too—don't think that he hasn't. You're not the only one who lost Mario that night.'

Valentina's own sense of building guilt mixed with her mother's gentle admonition made her unbearably prickly. She turned to face her. 'Did he, Mama? Did he really suffer? What about when he was cavorting on yachts in the south of France? Or making millions off the rich and idle gamblers in Europe? Or perhaps he suffered when he was staggering out of casinos at dawn in Monte Carlo with a bimbo model on each arm?'

It took Valentina a second to notice that her face had gone pale. 'Mama?'

Her mother was looking over her head and the hairs went up on the back of Valentina's neck. Slowly she turned to see a grim-faced Gio standing behind her. He had a bunch of flowers in his hand. Valentina gulped. He stepped up beside her, a face like thunder, and handed the flowers to Valentina's mother. And then he looked at Valentina, eyes so dark they looked black.

He took her arm and bit out, 'You and I need to talk.' And then he was pulling her unceremoniously from the clinic. Fear and trepidation was uppermost in Valentina's belly now, not even anger, although she'd never let Gio know that. She'd never seen him so angry. When they were outside he all but flung her arm away from him and faced her. Six foot two of bristling angry male, muscles rippling. He was a sight to behold.

Valentina backed away. 'I'm not going to talk to you when you're like this.'

'When I'm like what?' he almost roared. 'You barely talk to me any which way. I can't do anything right.'

Suddenly a wave of emotion came over her and terrified he'd see it in her eyes Valentina walked quickly to her car which was nearby. She heard a muffled curse but got in quickly and locked her doors. She was trembling all over when she pulled out of her car space and it got worse when she hit the open road and saw a familiar dark silver sports car behind her with a broad-shouldered figure at the wheel.

Gio was following her. It had an immediate effect on her body. A wave of heat made tiny beads of sweat break out over her top lip and between her breasts underneath her shirt. Her hands were sweaty on the wheel and her little car wheezed and panted as she pushed it over the speed limit. She ignored Gio flashing his lights behind her. All she knew was that she had to get away from him. Her emotions were far too volatile to deal with him right now. She felt as if she was on the edge of a precipice.

When she pulled into a space at the racetrack with a screech of brakes a few minutes later, Gio was right behind her. He slammed on his breaks too, sending up a shower of gravel and dust. He sprang out of his car, ripping off dark glasses. 'What the hell do you think you're playing at? You could have caused an accident!'

Valentina was shaking with all the strong emotions running through her. 'You know all about accidents, Corretti, don't you? Just stay away from me.'

He sneered. 'Oh, it's like that, is it? We've gone about two steps forward and three hundred back?'

Valentina clenched her hands to fists, her blood thumping in her head, making it spin. 'I quit, Corretti, OK? This isn't working. I should never have come to you in the first place.'

She started to stride away towards her accommodation fully intending to pack and leave and then felt a much larger presence beside her. He took her arm in his hand.

Again. It was too much; she yanked free and glared up into his face. 'Don't touch me.'

Suddenly Valentina became belatedly aware of people stopped in their tracks around them, watching avidly. Gio noticed too. Grimly he took her hand instead, in a grip so tight it bordered on being painful, and said, 'Not another word, Ferranti. We're taking this somewhere private. We are not done.'

Valentina was tight-lipped and white-faced by the time Gio was opening a door on the same floor as his offices. Her hand was still clamped in his and the way his much larger hand engulfed hers was far too disturbing. He finally let her go when he opened the door and all but pushed her through. She snatched back her hand and held it to her chest; it was tingling.

Pacing away from him, she was so pumped up that she barely noticed what was a very starkly designed yet luxurious small apartment. Minimal furnishings in soft greys and muted colours in the living area led into a bedroom and what she presumed to be a bathroom en suite.

Gio closed the door behind him and she heard him turn a key in the lock. Valentina backed away, eyes huge on him, instantly her sense of threat spiked. 'What do you think you're doing?'

Gio was grim. 'We're not leaving here until we've come to some agreement as to how to proceed without you wanting to rip my head off at every opportunity. It doesn't make for a good professional relationship.'

He crossed his arms. 'And first things first, you are *not* quitting.'

Valentina crossed her arms too. She was valiantly ignoring the fact that she was now alone in a locked room with

Gio Corretti and there was enough electricity crackling between them to light up the whole stadium.

'I can quit if I want to.'

Gio arched a brow. 'Really? Have you already forgotten that you came to me as a last resort?'

Valentina flushed. She had forgotten for a moment. She thought she had freedom. But she didn't. If she left now she couldn't allow Gio to pay for her parents' care and she'd be right back to square one. And it would be so much worse because she'd be decimating her father's chances of getting well again. It was inconceivable that she could do that to them.

'Fine.' She felt like a fool. 'I won't quit.'

Gio's brow got higher. 'That's big of you—after that little public display of animosity I would have grounds to fire you if I so wished.'

Fear lanced Valentina. She looked at Gio properly. 'But you just said that I couldn't quit.'

Gio looked at Valentina and suddenly the bravado was gone and she looked achingly young and vulnerable. Her hair had been tied up in a ponytail but long tendrils had come loose and drifted about her shoulders. She was wearing tight black skinny jeans, flat shoes and a white button-down shirt. It was slightly too short and he could see a sliver of pale flat belly underneath.

She wore no make-up and she was the most beautiful woman Gio had ever seen. A shaft of desire hit him right in the solar plexus, spreading outwards to every cell in his body, even as the realisation that he could never have her failed to douse that desire. It only served to rouse it.

Anger made Gio spit out, 'Let's get to the real issue here, the elephant in the room—*Mario*.'

He saw how Valentina blanched and her eyes got bigger. He pushed down the urge to apologise. Saying his name out loud was like exploding a soft yet lethal bomb between them. 'Come on,' he sneered. 'Aren't you just waiting for another opportunity to hurl some more insults and accusations my way?'

Perhaps it was the easy forgiveness of Valentina's parents working on him subconsciously, but for the first time in a long time, Gio actually felt a subtle shift in his ever-present sense of guilt. It wasn't so black or all-encompassing.

Valentina was struggling to hold on to something real, tangible. Her hatred for this man, for what he had done. She clung to it now like a drowning person clinging to a buoy. Her voice shook with tension. 'Don't you dare mention his name.'

Gio looked fearsome, his face tight with anger, eyes blazing. Muscles popping in his jaw. 'I have as much of a right to mention his name as you do.'

Valentina shook her head. 'No, no, you don't, you—'

'I what?' Gio cut in. 'I *killed him*? Is that what you're going to say?'

Emotion, thick and acrid and cloying, was rising up within Valentina, but it wasn't the easily understood grief for her brother. *That* she recognised and knew well; this was something much more ambiguous and disturbing. It was something to do with this man and how he made her feel, how he'd always made her feel.

Not understanding this visceral feeling he effortlessly evoked within her and hating him for it, Valentina suddenly flew at him with her hands balled to fists. She took him by surprise and he fell back against the door with a thump. His arms came around her to protect them both just as she registered that his chest was like steel under her hands. And, in the same instance, that she wanted to unfurl her hands and run them up over his muscles and not beat him.

Valentina sprang back, breaking his hold, aghast at her bubbling emotions. She was breathing hard and she looked up at Gio, who straightened up carefully from the door, hands behind him. His polo shirt strained over his hard chest. He was breathing hard too, his chest rising and falling. Tension was even thicker now between them along that ever-present crackle of electricity.

She was suddenly desperate to cling on to something, *anything* that could keep a distance between them, because for a moment it had fallen away. Dissolved in a rush of heat. Dissolved by the shocking extent of her awareness of him.

Valentina turned away for a moment to try and collect herself when she felt as if she was coming apart and then turned back, her control flimsy. 'You might not have killed him but you're responsible.'

A stillness seemed to surround Gio now, making Valentina even more nervous. When he spoke he sounded weary. 'And how long are you going to keep punishing me for that? Don't you think I've been punishing myself for it?'

Valentina tried to ignore the way something in his voice caused an ache inside her. She emitted a hoarse laugh and put out a hand to encompass their general surroundings. 'You call this punishment? Living in luxury? Making millions? Cavorting on yachts with celebrities?'

Gio's face got even starker and inwardly Valentina quivered. She had to concede uncomfortably that it had been some time since he'd been pictured on the hedonistic social scene. It had all ended abruptly after those couple of years, when he'd returned to Sicily and immersed himself in his racetrack. He hadn't even been pictured with a woman since then.

He came closer to her and she fought not to move back, every muscle screaming with tension. She felt as if she'd woken a slumbering lion.

'For two years I lived like that and it was no fun.'

'That's not the impression you gave to the world.' Valentina ignored the little voice of conscience that reminded her that Gio hadn't looked *happy* in any of the photos she'd seen of him in the press. He'd looked intense, as if driven by something.

Now Gio emitted a curt laugh that made Valentina flinch. He put a hand through his hair and stalked away from her to stand looking out the window with his back to her. Finally Valentina could breathe again. Every line of his body was taut. Shoulders broad, leading down to slim hips in low-riding worn jeans. Even now, in the midst of this high emotion, her attention was wandering, gaze captivated by his perfect backside, those powerful thighs and long legs.

Disgusted with herself, she swallowed back a curse and crossed her arms and lifted her gaze to the back of that dark head. And something inexplicably tender lanced her. She didn't have time to question it before Gio started talking in a cool voice.

'I ran away from here, something I'm not proud of.'

He turned around then and Valentina sucked in a breath at the bleakness on his face, in his eyes. 'If I could have been the one to die, do you not think I wished it a million times? Every time I woke up in the morning? I knew what I had done...I *know*. If we hadn't been friends, if I hadn't badgered him into coming out that night, if I hadn't had that damaged horse at my stables...' He broke off and then continued huskily. 'Do you not think I know that Mario's death was my fault? If I hadn't been arrogant enough to assume I could tame the most untameable of horses…Mario wouldn't have wanted to try himself, to prove me wrong.'

Bitterness laced Gio's voice now. 'I came from a life of excess I hadn't even earned, from a family connected only by their disconnectedness. Mario came from everything that was good and real.'

His eyes seemed to be skewering Valentina to the spot. She couldn't move. His voice roughened. 'The night Mario died…I went back to the palazzo and put Black Star down, even though he was physically uninjured. He *was* untameable, there *was* something wrong in his head, or genes, but I'd let him live. *Me*. He should have been put down months before, when that jockey had died.'

Gio's mouth was impossibly flat. 'It took another death before I saw through my sheer arrogance. When I left here I wanted to die too. I wanted to kill myself but that would have been too easy, too self-serving. So I did everything imaginable to court death, without it actually being by my hand.

'I jumped out of planes, I climbed impossible mountains, I went to war-torn regions in Africa—ostensibly for charity purposes but secretly hoping I'd find myself a target of some drug-crazed faction.'

Something cold went down Valentina's spine when she thought of the cavalier way in which Gio had played with his life.

But he wasn't finished. His mouth twisted in evident self-disgust. 'Instead I found myself being lauded as a champion of philanthropists, and became a pin-up for extreme-sport enthusiasts. So then I immersed myself in the debauched and shallow world of the truly idle and rich. Because that's what I deserved.'

He laughed curtly. 'After all, isn't that what I was? I'd never done a decent day's work in school and yet Mario, with infinitely less resources, had succeeded against all the odds. Do you not think that I *know* how much Mario's life was worth over mine?'

Valentina felt as if she'd just been punched in the gut with his words. She even put a hand there as if she could stop pain from blooming outwards. She couldn't say anything though, too stunned, too shocked....

Gio continued in a flat voice. 'The days were meaningless and morphed into one another, interspersed with whatever my next desperate flirtation with death would be. I lost and won back my entire fortune in the space of twenty-four hours many times over. One night in a casino I was so drunk I could barely see straight, but I was about to use Misfit as collateral in a bet with a renowned and very ruthless gambler. He'd been waiting for his moment to get my horse.

'And right then, I truly didn't care about Misfit, I didn't care about anything. I'd slept with a woman the night before and couldn't have even told you her name. She was just one of many.'

Valentina was silent. In shock. Not disgusted. Everything about him spoke of his own self-recrimination. She found herself inexplicably understanding his need to lose himself in something, anything.

Gio's mouth tightened, even as one corner turned up imperceptibly. 'It was in that moment, as I was about to let everything I'd ever cared about go, that I heard Mario's voice as clearly as if he were standing here now, in this room. He just said, *Enough*. And somehow…I got up and walked away.'

He looked directly at her. 'So no, those two years were not fun. I was living the empty life of an even emptier hedonist. I was half alive but not as dead as I wanted to be.'

Gio's words sank in and choked Valentina's vocal

chords. She believed his wish to die; she'd seen it on his face that day at the graveside and she'd welcomed it at the time because she had wanted to hurt him as she hurt. Yet only now she was realising how etched into her memory it had always been.

Helpless tears pricked her eyes at the thought of Mario's presence coming to Gio like that. She believed that too, because she'd felt him around her at certain times. It's exactly what he would have said to Gio.

Overcome and floundering badly at Gio's emotionally stark confession that gave her no room to attack him, Valentina put her hands to her face to hide her blurring vision as if that could hide the emotion that was rising like a dam breaking deep inside her. She faintly heard a sound and felt Gio's presence come closer and suddenly Valentina could do nothing but obey a deep need and instinctively she reached for Gio, wrapping her arms blindly around his waist. Within seconds she was sobbing into his chest.

For a long moment he did nothing and Valentina knew she was clinging to him like a limpet but she couldn't stop it. And then slowly, his arms came around her and he was holding her so tight she thought her bones might crush. She cried for a long time, until little hiccups were coming out of her mouth. She'd cried for Mario so many times she'd lost count, but this was infinitely different. There was something cathartic about this.

When the hiccups had stopped and Valentina's breaths evened out again, she felt wrung out but also very aware of being held so tightly in Gio's arms. Her breasts were crushed to his belly and her nipples were tight and hard against the lace of her bra. Sensitised and tingling.

The material of Gio's shirt was damp under her wet cheek and she could feel the delineation of hard muscle, the rise and fall of his chest. His heartbeat was slightly fast under her cheek, his scent musky and earthy. And down lower, where her hips were all but welded to his hard thighs, Valentina could feel his arousal pressing into her soft belly.

This realisation didn't shame her or disgust her. It excited her, and thrilled her. She didn't want to move, or breathe. Didn't want to break the spell that seemed to hover over them. It was as if the intense flood of emotion had washed something acrid away.

Finally, reluctantly, Valentina pulled back within Gio's arms. She couldn't stay welded to him forever.

His hold slackened fractionally and she looked up. His face was stark, intent. She could still feel him, rigid against her, and she wanted to move her hips. Her sex tingled in response and her heart thumped because she knew she wanted this man. No other man had ever managed to touch or arouse this very secret part of her.

Gio lifted his arms and brought his hands to Valentina's face, cupping her jaw, his thumbs wiping away the moisture from her cheeks. She knew she must look a sight, and Gio's shirt had to be sodden from her tears and runny nose. But she didn't care. A fierce burgeoning desire was rising within her, something which had been there before but had been put on ice for seven years.

For a long time it had been illicit and forbidden, *guilty*. But from the moment she'd seen him again it had flamed to life. Yet the contradiction had duelled within her: how could she hate him and want him at the same time? But now those questions faded in her head. *Hate* felt like a much more indefinable thing and the desire was there, stronger than hate, rushing through her blood and making her feel alive.

She lifted a hand and touched Gio's hard jaw. He clenched it against her hand. Desire thickened the air around them, unmistakable. As if questioning it, Gio looked down at her, a small frown between his eyes. 'Valentina?'

It was the same look he'd given her the other night when she'd exposed herself and she understood it now. He'd been asking the question then, unsure of what she'd been telling him with her body language. The knowledge was heady. He *wanted* her.

One of Valentina's fingers touched Gio's bottom lip, tracing its full sensuous outline. Words were rising up within her, she couldn't keep them back. 'Gio…kiss me.' She'd wanted this, *ached* for this, for so long.

It was only after an interminable moment of nothing happening that she looked up into Gio's eyes and saw something like torture in their dark green depths. He shook his head. 'This is not a good idea. You don't want this, not really.'

Gio heard himself say the words and felt his erection straining against his jeans, against her soft curves. He'd never felt harder in his life and it had nothing to do with being celibate for five years. He wanted to kiss and plunder this woman before she changed her mind but he knew he couldn't. She hated him already; she would despise him for ever for this.

Valentina's gaze narrowed on his. A light was dawning in her eyes. He braced himself for the moment when she would pull herself free and demand to know what the hell he was doing.

And then she said, 'Damn you, Gio Corretti, *kiss me.*'

Had she really said those words? Valentina looked up at Gio, the question screaming in her head, *Why won't he just kiss me?* She could feel his erection, even harder now, and imagined it straining against his jeans, against her.

She felt damp heat moisten between her legs. Desperation wasn't far away and suddenly it hit her: she was a warm female body who had all but thrown herself at him. Few men *wouldn't* respond to that.

Horrified to think that she'd so badly misread the situation, very belatedly she tried to move, to get free of Gio's embrace, but suddenly his hands tightened on her jaw, fingers reaching around to her neck.

Gio had had a moment of doubt when she'd uttered those words. *Damn you, Gio Corretti, kiss me.* He thought he'd been hallucinating. But then she hadn't moved away; she'd looked up at him with a distinctive light of determination in her eyes. And more than that, he'd seen the stark need in those amber depths. Unmistakable. The same need he felt right now.

But then he'd seen the flicker of doubt and uncertainty cross her face. Clearly she thought he didn't want her when such a thought was laughable. Couldn't she *feel* his need straining against her? Gio knew a stronger man would take the opportunity to push her back. A more moral man would tell her to go and not take advantage of this heightened moment. But he was not that man. He'd been damned a long time ago and he wanted Valentina.

All he could think of now was of the lovers she must have already had and jealousy burnt up his spine. A woman as beautiful as her, the kind of woman who had just demanded he kiss her—she wasn't innocent. And he couldn't bear to think of her with anyone else. He wanted her to want only him. Think of only him.

And she did want him. A fierce exultant force rushed through him and it was so strong that Gio had to control it with effort. She was moving in earnest now, trying to get away and a fierce primitive force surged through him, making his hands tighten. He growled softly, 'Where do you think you're going?'

Valentina's breath hitched and she looked into his eyes. Gio was responding now; his eyes were slumberous and blazing. His need was laid bare for her to see, as if she hadn't already felt it in his body, and while one part of her exulted, another part contracted. Suddenly she felt out of her depth.

'I…I changed my mind,' she said almost hopefully, even as her treacherous body was responding to the heat in Gio's eyes, the way his body felt next to hers.

He shook his head slowly and Valentina felt herself being mesmerised. 'It's too late for that. You asked to be kissed and so I'm going to kiss you.'

His hands were tight around her jaw, fingers caressing the back of her head. Valentina felt completely exposed and vulnerable as Gio's head started to descend. Intense flutters of excitement and anticipation shot through her abdomen and she had the stark realisation of how much she'd always longed for this moment. She wasn't strong enough to pull away and she wasn't sure Gio would even let her go.

There was a feral intensity in his eyes as his head dipped closer and closer and, like a coward, Valentina let her eyes drift shut. When his mouth finally touched hers, the sensation of those hard sensual contours was so exquisite against her sensitive lips that she had to grab on to his T-shirt to hold on.

His touch was hard, but gentle. Exploratory. Valentina was aware of his hands moving, thumbs trailing across her jaw as his hands went to the back of her head, where he found and pulled out her hairband. She could feel her hair falling around her shoulders, and one of Gio's big hands cradled the back of her head, angling her so that he could move his mouth on hers with lazy expert sensuality.

Valentina only realised she wasn't breathing when Gio coaxed her mouth to open to his, his tongue touching the seam of her lips. When she drew in a breath the full reality of kissing Gio Corretti hit her like a steam train. His scent hit her nostrils, even muskier now, laden with the promise of something so carnal that her toes curled.

His hand tightened on her head, and his other hand found its way to her back, pulling her into him, arching her spine. And it wasn't enough. As their tongues touched, Valentina pressed even closer.

The sensation of tongues touching and tasting, exploring, was so exquisite that Valentina never wanted it to stop. Everything was heightened. Valentina was aware of how hard his arousal felt, pressing into her. Restlessly, her hips moved, and as if in answer Gio's hand went to her hip, where he flattened it across the small of her back, pressing her in even tighter.

When she felt the faintly calloused skin of the palm of his hand against the bare skin just above the waist of her jeans she only knew that she wanted *more*.

His hand drifted up to her bra strap and Valentina's breasts seemed to swell and tighten in response, she broke away from the kiss. She opened her eyes to look up into those dark green depths. Her mouth felt swollen, bruised. Her heart was thundering and she felt dizzy. She realised that she was on her tippy-toes; her arms were tight around Gio's neck and she was so close to his mouth that their breaths intermingled. If she could have climbed into his skin right then she would have done it without hesitation.

Gio's hand was spread flat across Valentina's smooth back; her skin was like silk. Her bra strap was a provocative inducement to just flip it open, slide his hands around and cup those firm swells. His whole body *ached* with want.

Somehow he managed to get out, 'Do you want this?'

Valentina was aware of what Gio was asking. This wouldn't end with just this kiss. If she said yes, it would be everything. All of her. There were voices in her head urging her to stop, think. But they were dim. Stronger was the urgent primal desire she felt. This man and this moment was all she could focus on. She wanted him with a hunger that was completely alien and new to her, and she couldn't walk away from it. Right then she seriously doubted the ability of her legs to hold her up anyway. Gio was all but holding her up.

Slowly Valentina nodded her head. 'Yes, I want this.'

Looking slightly tortured Gio just asked, 'Are you sure?'

He was giving her a chance to go, to think about this. Her heart lurched. She nodded again and said firmly, 'Yes.'

Valentina was lifted into Gio's arms against his chest so fast that her head swam. He shouldered his way into the bedroom off the main living area and Valentina could see a huge bed dressed in dark grey linen. The sun was setting outside, bathing the room in a dusky glow.

'What is this place?' she asked far too belatedly, a little stunned at how fast everything was moving.

'It's mine, sometimes I stay overnight.'

Gio carefully lowered her to stand by the bed. For the first time in what felt like aeons there was space between them and already Valentina felt bereft. It scared her. But not enough to put more space between them.

Gio's face was flushed and the first indication of stubble darkened his jaw. He opened his mouth and Valentina quickly put her hand up to cover it, afraid he was going to ask her again if she knew what she was doing. She didn't want to think or rationalise what was happening. She just wanted to feel.

Gio took her hand down and a small smile touched his

mouth as if he understood. He held her hand against his chest where she could feel his heartbeat fast but strong, and with his other hand he wrapped it around her neck and pulled her towards him.

This time the kiss was hungry and devouring. It became heated in seconds, and Valentina curled her hand into his shirt, bunching it up. Her other hand went to his hip and found the hot skin underneath his shirt. Emboldened, she slid it around to his back and explored under his jeans, feeling the cleft of his smooth buttocks. Gio broke the kiss and said thickly, 'I need to see you.'

His hands were on her shirt, undoing her buttons. Valentina shivered with anticipation and looked down. Gio's hands looked huge and very dark, long fingers grappling with tiny buttons. She heard him curse softly when the buttons eluded his grasp and brought her own hands up to do the job. To be standing here, undressing in front of Gio…it was too huge to think about.

When her shirt fell open to reveal her lacy bra, Valentina blushed hotly. Gio pushed her hands aside and pulled open the shirt even more, until it came off her shoulders and down her arms and fell to the floor.

She couldn't look up at him. A hand snaked around to her back and undid her bra. He pulled the two straps down her arms and her bra joined her shirt on the floor. Instinctively Valentina went to cover her breasts but Gio stopped her arms. 'Don't…'

He tipped up her chin so that she had to look at him and his eyes were molten with heat and need, dissolving Valentina's inhibitions. 'You're beautiful.'

She saw his eyes drop to take in the swells of her breasts and their tips tingled painfully. With two hands he cupped them, and moved his thumbs across the sensitised peaks.

Valentina moaned softly, closing her eyes. It was too much to see his hands on her flesh like that.

Somehow Gio manoeuvred them so that he was sitting on the bed and he brought Valentina between his hard thighs, trapping her between them. With one hand on her waist holding her steady, he cupped a breast with his other and brought his mouth forward, and fed that hungry aching tip into the hot cavern of his mouth. Valentina sucked in a tortured breath and her hands went to his shoulders, holding on for dear life as shards of intense pleasure went from her nipple to between her legs.

Gio was remorseless, sucking and teasing the peak into throbbing stiffness. Flicking it with this tongue before sucking fiercely again. Valentina wasn't even aware of her hand going to the back of his head to hold him there. She cried out when he moved to the other breast and administered the same exquisite torture. Valentina had never known a pleasure like it. It was awakening an even more intense need in her body, down low, where her legs were pressed together by Gio's thighs.

Suddenly Valentina pulled back from his wicked mouth and looked down. Her eyelids felt heavy. Thickly she muttered, 'I want to see you too.' And she bent down to pull Gio's polo shirt up and over his head. When his magnificent torso was revealed she could only look at it as reverently as he'd looked at her.

He was beautifully muscled, not an ounce of fat. Dark olive skin and a very masculine dusting of hair. Gio's eyes glittered fiercely and he said, 'Come here.'

Valentina obeyed without question but this time she straddled Gio's thighs so that she was sitting on his lap. He brought both arms around her and the sensation of her bare breasts and wet nipples against his chest made her gasp. He pulled her head down to his and covered her mouth, swallowing her gasp. Her arousal levels rose to fever pitch. She'd never known there could be so many kinds of kisses. This was dark and wicked and she could feel the bulge of his erection underneath the apex of her legs. She wriggled, heightening the sensation. Gio's hand went to the front of her jeans and Valentina broke off the kiss with a gasp when she felt his fingers come between her jeans and skin.

Her hair was falling down her back, making every nerve end stand on edge. Gio's fingers were hot against her lower belly and as she looked into his eyes he flicked his thumb and opened the top button. With the top button gaping open and the zip pulled down, Gio spread his hand around the back of her waist and delved underneath, cupping one firm buttock.

Valentina arched upwards against him, and Gio took advantage, his mouth and tongue unerringly finding a turgid nipple and sucking fiercely as his hand went deeper and his fingers found the damp cleft of her body.

Valentina cried out, her legs pressing tight against his thighs as if that might assuage the delicious torture, but then suddenly the earth was moving and she was on her back on the bed with Gio looming over her, his shoulders impossibly broad, a lock of dark hair falling messily onto his forehead.

Valentina wanted to reach up to touch that lock, invaded by a dangerous tenderness, and had to clench her hand to a fist to stop it. Thankfully Gio was far too busy distracting her to see anything of this turmoil within her.

With a fast economy of movement he had opened her jeans fully and was pulling them down and off so now she was in nothing but her knickers. This was more naked than she'd ever been in front of anyone apart from her mother and Valentina bit her lip when trepidation and insecurity lanced her.

Something pierced through the heat haze in Gio's brain when he saw the flicker of trepidation on Valentina's face, and the full plumpness of her bottom lip caught between small white teeth. Like a cold bucket of water being thrown in his face, something occurred to him. His hands stilled on the button of his jeans and he frowned. 'Valentina… are you a virgin?'

CHAPTER SIX

GIO SAW VALENTINA'S face flush and a heavy weight settled in his gut. She brought up an arm to cover her breasts and just like that the temperature in the room zoomed down from about a million degrees to minus forty.

Stifling an almost overwhelming urge to smash his fist into the nearest solid object, Gio stepped back from the sinful provocation of Valentina's practically naked supine body. A body he would have been sinking into right now and discovering for himself just how innocent she was, with scant thought of being gentle.

On stiff legs he went straight to the bathroom and lifted the robe from the back of the door and came back, holding it out to Valentina, who he avoided looking at on the bed. Discovering she was innocent was not something he'd expected in a million years and this changed everything. She could not really want him to be the one to take her innocence, and when the heat of passion died away, she'd realise that and hate him even more.

'What are you doing?' Her voice, soft and husky, grated over his exposed and sensitive nerves. The muscles in his arm bunched and he said more curtly than he intended, 'Take the robe, Valentina, I don't sleep with virgins.'

Valentina was sitting up on the bed holding the robe to her naked chest, in shock, for a long minute afterwards. Gio had left the room, pulling on his shirt as he did with just a curt, 'I'll wait outside.'

She felt cold all over and yet still hot and tingly inside. The sense of something momentous being ripped out of her grasp was huge. There was an awful sting to his rejection of her because she was a virgin, a sting that cut much deeper than she liked to acknowledge. To avoid looking at that far too controversial subject, Valentina allowed anger to rise into her overheated brain. How dared Gio react like that?

The anger gave her the impetus to move and with stiff arms she pulled on the robe and belted it tightly around her and stalked out to the living area. When she emerged it was to see the rigid lines of Gio's body as he looked out the window with his back to her. He clearly knew she was there as she saw him tense even more.

Valentina resisted the urge to pick something up and fling it at his head. Instead she said with saccharine sweetness, 'I'll just go and divest myself of my virginity and be back so we can continue where we left off, shall I?'

Gio whirled around, arms crossed and muscles bunched. Tension stamped all over his features. He looked wild and uncivilised and it made Valentina feel even hotter.

'You should have been honest with me.'

Valentina crossed her arms and laughed out loud. 'You are such a hypocrite! You just told me that you've slept with women and not even remembered their names—how do you know that they weren't virgins?'

Gio winced. Why on earth had he spilled his guts like that? He'd never articulated to anyone how empty and meaningless those two years were. How low he'd sunk.

He tried to ignore how achingly sexy Valentina looked in nothing but the robe with her dark hair spread out across her shoulders. Frustration coursed through his veins, making his body hurt. He bit out, 'They weren't. Believe me.'

Valentina taunted, 'So I should preface every kiss I have with a man with "By the way I'm a virgin"?'

Something dark went into Gio's gut at the thought of her kissing any other man. 'Yes, especially if every kiss ends up with you lying half naked on a bed.'

Valentina sucked in a gasp at the injustice of that comment and felt the prickle of humiliating tears. All she could think of right then was how ardently she'd thrown herself at Gio, how she'd begged him to kiss her. Make love to her. She'd been gyrating on his lap like some kind of an exotic dancer. He'd tried to stop her, had asked her twice if she wanted this, and each time she'd said a resounding *yes*.

As if sensing her turmoil Gio uncrossed his arms and put out a hand. Valentina backed away and fire raced up her spine, obliterating any lingering desire. 'I hate you, Giacomo Corretti. And I wouldn't sleep with you now if you were the last man on this earth.'

Valentina whirled around and hated that tears were blurring her vision. She dashed them away and went back into the bedroom where she ripped off the robe and dragged on her clothes, every move she'd made and kiss she'd just given this man running through her head like a bad B-movie.

When she re-emerged she stalked straight to the main door, turned the key and had her hand on the handle before she felt a hand on her other arm. Instantly sensations ran all the way down to her groin and her still-sensitive breasts peaked.

'Look, Valentina, wait—'

She ripped her arm free and looked up into Gio's face. The contrition she saw there sent her over the edge. She could handle anything but not this...*pity*. She lifted a hand and before she was even aware of the impulse, it had connected so hard with his face that his head snapped around. Trembling all over from an overdose of adrenalin and emotion she said, 'Don't touch me again. *Ever.*'

The first day of the Corretti Cup race meeting was dawning and Gio stood in his study office looking out the window at the hive of activity in every corner of the racetrack. It was usually his favourite time of the year but this year he was impossibly distracted. Distracted by a five-foot-seven chestnut-haired, amber-eyed temptress and a level of sexual frustration he'd never known could exist. Not to mention the ever-simmering cauldron of emotions in his gut—ever since he'd seen her again. Gone was the numb shell that had been encasing him since he'd returned to Sicily.

Valentina.

Her name was on his mind, his lips, every waking moment. He could still feel the sting of her hand across his face. It had been no less than he'd deserved.

When he'd realised she was a virgin he'd reacted viscerally. He could never be the one to take that prize from her. It would be a travesty. Yet she had been ready to give it—in the heat of the moment. Gio knew damn well that in the aftermath Valentina would have realised the magnitude of what she'd just done and with *who*, and she would have felt nothing but disgust for giving in to such base desires.

Grief for Mario—talking about him had defused something between them, but no way was it strong enough to withstand the bitter and deep anger she undoubtedly still felt towards Gio. The chemistry that sizzled between them had obscured that momentarily.

She might hate him for rejecting her now, but he'd saved him and her from that simmering enmity deepening even more.

Gio knew all this and repeated it over and over again

to himself but the truth was that he was lying to himself. Because for all of his lofty assertions to Valentina that he didn't sleep with virgins, all he wanted to do was close the gates to his racetrack, turn everyone away, find her and put her over his shoulder like a caveman. And then he wanted to take her to a quiet place and make love to her until they were both weak and sated.

Until she was no longer a virgin. Until she was *his* and no one else's.

Valentina should have been focusing on the task at hand— the first day of the Corretti Cup—but her mind kept veering off track back to the other evening and the excruciating humiliation of having Gio reject her because she was a virgin.

Even now, hot tears pricked her eyes and to counteract the weak emotion she stabbed a fork with unnecessary zeal into a piece of pork. She felt so conflicted...the hate she'd always felt for Gio was disturbingly elusive now. She wanted to think of his rejection, hold that to her like a cold justification, but she kept thinking about what he'd told her.

He'd ripped apart a huge part of her defence around him by revealing what he'd gone through after Mario's death.

And then he'd taken her in his arms...and Valentina had turned into a complete stranger. She'd *begged* him to kiss her, to make love to her. Self-disgust filled her now. Few men would turn that down...and Gio had merely proved himself as susceptible to a warm willing body as the next man. What he hadn't counted on was her unwelcome innocence.

The hurt that seized her in the pit of her belly reminded Valentina that his rejection had cut far deeper than she wanted to acknowledge.

Stabbing the pork viciously again, Valentina told herself

that he'd done her a favour by not sleeping with her. Her
conscience pricked her to think of the emotional fall-out
if she *had* slept with him and for the first time she consid-
ered the rogue idea that perhaps he'd done it out of some
moral sense of integrity.

One thing was certain: there was no way that Valentina
was ever going to allow him to make her feel so vulnerable or exposed again.

'Val?'

Valentina looked up feeling a little dazed to see her assistant Sara, who was eyeing the very overpierced piece
of pork warily.

'Yes?'

Sara looked up. 'I, ah, just checked the main buffet tent
and it's all moving like clockwork. No one is waiting for
their food.'

Valentina forced a smile and her mind back to the task
at hand with effort. 'Thanks, Sara, I'll go and check the
VIP tent. You can start to organise the canapés for the
drinks reception later.'

As Valentina hurried off she forced all thoughts of Gio
out of her head but then she suddenly caught a glimpse of
him in the distance and instantly all efforts to put him out
of her head were reduced to naught. She cursed loudly.

'You look stunning tonight.'

The tiny hairs rose all over Valentina's body and her
breath automatically quickened and her heart missed a
beat. She looked up from where she was running a pen
down the list of VIP names to see Gio standing in front
of her, ludicrously handsome in his black tuxedo. He'd
changed since she'd caught that sighting of him earlier.
His normally unruly hair was tamed into some kind of
order, making him look even more debonair.

She'd been burningly aware of him since he'd walked into the huge and lavishly decorated marquee about an hour before but to her relief he'd been on the other side of the room, talking to people. Mainly a steady stream of women which had aroused very dark and disturbing feelings inside her. But now he was here. And she couldn't breathe.

Somehow she found the wherewithal to breathe in and said coolly, 'It's the only formal dress I have—I didn't have time to go shopping.'

Gio's dark eyes ran over her from where she'd put her hair up in a simple high knot, down over the black structured dress with its flared skirt and a pair of peep-toe black shoes. She was markedly dressed down compared to all the other women in the room who were dripping in jewels and dressed in the latest slinky silky fashions. Which was only appropriate, she'd told herself, hating that she felt somehow *less*.

Despite the vivid recall of the other night and her lingering sense of humiliation and anger, Valentina felt hot colour seeping up her chest when face to face with Gio again and the memory of how she'd slapped him. She'd never hit another human being in her life. The compulsion to apologise was suddenly acute. Her emotions had betrayed her and she didn't want him to think she still felt so volatile. Avoiding his eyes, she said stiffly, 'I'm sorry... about hitting you.'

'I deserved it.'

Gio's quick answer had her looking up to see him put a hand to his jaw as if to test it. Her belly clenched when she noticed a tiny scar high on his cheekbone. Had she done that? Treacherously her intent to be cool dissolved. 'Did I really hurt you?'

Gio's mouth curled up on one side, making Valentina's insides feel curiously liquid.

'Let's just say I wouldn't want to be on the other end of your right hook.'

'I'm sorry,' she said again, her voice sounding frigid as she tried to disguise her emotions.

Just then a petite and very groomed dark-haired woman came up to Gio's side and he dipped his head to listen to what she had to say. The woman blushed prettily and something dark pierced Valentina's composure to see this evidence of another woman finding him attractive. *Attractive?* a snide voice in her head mocked—he stood head and shoulders above every other man in the room and she knew it.

The woman had moved away and Gio was looking at her. Valentina realised her hands were curled to fists and she consciously relaxed them.

Gio was saying smoothly, 'If you'll excuse me—my mother's father is looking for a recommendation for tomorrow's race.'

Valentina nodded her head vigorously, and Gio mocked softly but with an undefinable light in his eyes, 'You don't have to look so pleased to see me go.'

He walked away and Valentina couldn't help recalling the bleakness she'd seen the other evening, the way Gio had called himself *worthless*. He seemed to her to strike a poignantly lone figure amongst the teeming crowd.

To Valentina's relief she was kept too busy after that to think about Gio or where he was. And much later when she came up for air, he seemed to be firmly ensconced on the other side of the tent with the last of the guests. She was supervising the start of the clear-up. The jazz band that had been playing were putting their instruments away. Franco, her other assistant, came up to her and said, 'Why don't you take off? I'll make sure this is all done. You've got an early start tomorrow.'

Valentina smiled at her assistant ruefully and pointed out, 'So do you.'

But just then she saw Gio look over to where she was, and he stood up, before threading his way through the small tables with his easy leonine grace. Flutters of sensation erupted in her belly and she felt very vulnerable when she remembered the volatile mix of emotions this man had aroused earlier. He was getting closer. Her smile faded and she blurted out to Franco, 'Actually, I'd really appreciate that if you don't mind.'

Franco was assuring her it was fine but Valentina was already halfway out of the marquee and didn't look back to see how Gio's expression darkened to one of thunder as he took in her escape.

Gio stopped dead in the middle of the tent and watched as Valentina's slim back disappeared through the doorway. He cursed softly at his impulse to snatch her back. What was he going to do? Demand she wait until every last person had left? She'd been working more tirelessly than almost anyone else involved in the Cup and had made the first day a resounding success. More than one person had come to him to ask him who was doing the catering. The champagne reception had gone without a hitch. Her staff were more than capable of dealing with the clean-up.

He ran a hand through his hair and cursed again. The truth was, he had no interest in talking to her about the day, or business. He only wanted *her*. He'd thought earlier that something had softened between them when she'd apologised for hitting him. She'd looked genuinely contrite. But her words from that night came back to him now, ringing in his ears: *Don't touch me again. Ever.*

She'd just been polite and professional. That was all.

It didn't help that all evening he'd been acutely aware of her as she'd greeted guests at the door, a wide smile on her face. She'd stood out from the other women who looked like ridiculous birds of paradise—overdone and over-made-up—with the simplest of black dresses which had highlighted her slender figure. The V-neck design had allowed tantalising glimpses of her smooth pale cleavage and Gio had had to battle against the images of her bared breasts, nipples wet from his tongue, racing through his head at the least opportune moments.

An acquaintance, a renowned French playboy, had asked him earlier, 'Who is the stunning woman greeting us this evening?'

Gio had all but snarled at him, 'She's not available.' The intensity of emotion he'd felt as it had coursed through his blood had blindsided him. He'd wanted to grab the man by the neck and throw him out. As it was he'd watched him with an eagle eye all night.

His mouth tightened. Valentina might desire him but she would never allow him close again. And if he had a shred of conscience, he wouldn't touch her again. The problem was, Gio didn't think his conscience was strong enough to overcome the physical craving racing through his blood, or the possessiveness he felt.

The following afternoon Valentina went back to her rooms to change for the second evening's champagne reception. The second day had passed off as successfully as the first, so far, and she was finally allowing herself to relax a little. She'd even managed to stop for a moment earlier, while checking one of the corporate boxes, and had got swept up in the spine-tingling finish of the main race of the day.

The sheer scale of the event and amounts of money being bet and won made her eyes boggle. She'd never seen such luxe wealth in her life. And amongst all the excess had been Gio—surveying everything and everyone around him. More than once she'd seen him dip his head discreetly to one of his staff who would rush off and avert a potential crisis or situation. But what had struck her again more than anything was how *alone* he'd looked, and how that had made her feel.

One of her very first memories was of playing outside her father's workshop at the palazzo while Mario helped him inside, and watching the lone figure of a young Gio as he'd watched his father's stable hands exercise the horses on their gallops.

Just a couple of hours ago as she'd stood in the background with a tray of empty glasses, Valentina had had to suppress the almost overwhelming urge to put down her tray and go up to him and slip her hand into his. She'd found herself imagining him looking down at her and smiling back...and squeezing her hand.

The tray of glasses had been shaking in her hands before she'd come to her senses and rushed off again. And now as she let herself into her rooms she shook her head. What was wrong with her? Why was her mind taking such flights of fancy? She had to admit that her virulent anger had become something else, but it was not tender. No matter how many times that soft emotion seemed to be taking her unawares.

When Valentina had put down her bag and was in the centre of her room she noticed the clothes through the open bedroom door. She went in to see that there were two floor-length evening dresses and one shorter cocktail-length dress in clear protective covers hanging off the doors of her wardrobe. Lined up below were three pairs of shoes all colour coded to go with the dresses. Laid out on her bed she could see more bags and on her dresser she could see jewellery boxes.

Stunned, she walked closer. The dresses were gorgeous, the stuff of fantasy. One was dark red, another royal blue and the cocktail dress was strapless and black with a beaded lace overlay that made it sparkle.

She backed away and saw the boxes on the bed. Feeling a sense of dread she opened one and lifted back gold tissue paper to see the wispiest, most delicate underwear she'd ever seen in her life. Hurriedly she closed it back up again.

It was only then that she noticed the white square of paper with a typewritten message near the biggest box..

Valentina, I hope you don't mind that I took the liberty of ordering you some dresses. You'd mentioned that you hadn't had time to shop....

At the bottom of the note there was just a simple *G*.

First of all Valentina felt the predictable rise of hot rage—how dared Gio presume to buy her clothes? But then the note was so impersonal—he hadn't even written it by hand. He must have got his secretary to type it out.

Then her cheeks got hot with embarrassment. Had he thought she looked completely out of place last night in her chain-store dress? He'd told her she looked stunning but the truth was that he'd probably offered up that platitude to every woman there. She'd never catered for such a prestigious event before; she'd never had to dress up.

She saw her dress now, hanging where she'd left it last night on the back of the bedroom door, and it looked unbearably shabby and worn next to these designer concoctions of perfection. Her embarrassment levels went up a notch. Gio evidently didn't want her showing him up with his important guests and friends.

For a second intense vulnerability hit Valentina when she entertained the notion of putting one of these dresses on, and seeing Gio's reaction to her. Would he want her then? In spite of her unwelcome virginity? Did she want to seduce him?

Humiliation, never far, made hot colour seep up into her face and rebellion fired her blood as she ignored the beautiful creations and resolutely pulled on her own dress and shoes. Valentina pushed down the voice telling her she was being ridiculously childish and when she was ready she left her room to go back to work.

It was some hours later before Valentina felt the familiar tingle of awareness. Much to her chagrin, she'd just dropped a pen from nerveless fingers for about the tenth time that evening and was bending down to pick it up.

His impeccably polished shoes came into her line of vision and she sucked in a deep fortifying breath before straightening up.

Her mouth dried. Tonight Gio was wearing a white shirt and that white bow tie. It was slightly askew as if he'd been pulling at it impatiently, giving him a rakish air. Faint stubble lined his jaw. Valentina struggled to find her equilibrium, hating that he'd caught her before she had a chance to compose herself. And then she thought of the typed note and the dresses, and forced ice into her veins.

She hitched up her chin and said in her coolest voice, 'You didn't have to go to the trouble of sending someone out to buy me dresses. If you'd told me what was required I could have taken an hour to go out and buy something myself.'

Gio's eyes flashed with displeasure. 'The idea was that you choose one to wear tonight.'

Valentina welcomed the surge of anger and glanced

around to make sure no one was near before hissing at him, 'I'm not one of your mistresses, Gio.'

Gio opened his mouth to respond but suddenly they were interrupted by one of his aides, who Valentina dimly recognised as working on the equestrian side of things.

He was saying sotto voce, 'Excuse me Signor Corretti, but Sheikh Nadim of Merkazad has just arrived with his wife. I thought you'd want to know. We've settled his horses into the stables already.'

Valentina knew that Sheikh Nadim was one of the most important guests Gio had been expecting. She saw a muscle clench in Gio's jaw and felt quivery inside. He just looked at her for an intense moment and then bit out a curt, 'We'll continue this later.' And he strode off with his PA.

Valentina had little time to think about his thinly veiled threat because she was quickly swamped by more guests and making sure that everyone was being catered to, and that the champagne was kept flowing.

Much later, Gio was ripping open his bow tie and opening the top button of his shirt as he made his way to Valentina's rooms. It was long after everyone had finished up for the night.

Sheikh Nadim of Merkazad, an old friend of Gio's, had invited him back to his hotel for a nightcap and he hadn't been able to refuse. Gio usually loved any chance he got to talk about horses and racing with Nadim, but not this time. Eventually his friend had chuckled ruefully and said, 'I'll release you from your misery. Go and find her, my friend. I know that tortured look well. I saw it in my own mirror often enough.'

Gio shook his head now—he couldn't ever imagine when Nadim and his Irish wife, Iseult, hadn't been completely and soppily in love. In truth he found it hard to be around them—to witness that level of utter devotion and absorption. It made him feel all at once claustrophobic and yet curiously restless, yearning for something he couldn't articulate.

Ruthlessly pushing aside such incendiary lines of thought, Gio took the stairs now two at a time, his blood humming at the thought of seeing Valentina.

Valentina was still pacing in her room an hour after she'd returned from the empty marquee. Gio had disappeared at some stage and she hated the way she'd felt disappointed that he hadn't returned to explain whatever he'd meant by 'We'll continue this later.'

He'd obviously gone back to the luxurious hotel in Syracuse where most of the guests were staying, and where she knew there was an exclusive nightclub. Her hands curled to fists without her even realising it as she had a vision of Gio standing at the side of the dance floor with throbbing music and lights highlighting any number of beautiful women he could have within a mere flick of his fingers. *Experienced women.*

A peremptory knock sounded on her door and Valentina stopped dead, breath caught in her throat. Superstitiously she didn't move and it came again, along with a familiar voice that sounded positively angry. 'Valentina!'

Livid with herself for the relief she was feeling but also because she'd let him get to her so much she stalked to the door and said through it, 'It's late, Gio, what do you want?'

On the other side of the door Gio bit back the succinct answer he wanted to give: *you.* Instead he said, 'I told you I'd talk to you later.'

Valentina's voice, husky enough to set his nerve endings alight and yet cool enough to try, and fail, to douse them floated through. 'I'm tired and going to bed. We can talk tomorrow.'

Valentina had a sudden morbid fear of Gio coming through the door. The sting of rejection came back vividly. She knew if she was in close proximity to him she might not be able to disguise her far too disturbing emotions. Or the fact that she wanted him with a hunger that was shameful.

Gio's voice came back hard and implacable as the wood of the door. 'Either you let me in, Valentina, or I use the master key to let myself in.'

Valentina crossed her arms and hissed out, 'That's a blatant infringement of my employee rights. If you do any such thing I'll quit right now and sue you for harassment!'

The eloquent answer to that was the unmistakable sound of a key going into her lock and turning. The door opened to reveal a dark and dishevelled-looking Gio with bow tie hanging completely askew now, his jacket hanging off one finger. And Valentina felt the inevitable surge of electricity between them like a doom-laden klaxon going off.

He was in and the door was shut firmly behind him again before she'd recovered from the shock. Gio's dark eyes were running over her and he said throatily, 'We hadn't finished our discussion about your wardrobe.'

Those words returned Valentina to reality with a bump. She moved away, tightening her arms across her chest. 'I am not discussing this with you now. So if you don't mind…?'

Gio casually threw his jacket onto a nearby chair and leant back easily against the door, and looked at her. 'I don't mind at all—you can do what you like once we've finished our conversation.'

CHAPTER SEVEN

VALENTINA LOOKED FROM the strewn jacket to him and then turned and paced away, glad she'd at least taken off her shoes because her legs felt wobbly enough at the moment. She turned back, feeling seriously jittery now and threatened to have her private space invaded like this, especially when she thought of the frothy lace excuses for underwear in the boxes in the other room. 'I told you, Gio—I'm not one of your mistresses so please don't feel like you have to kit me out in a similar manner.'

Gio flushed and Valentina took a step back.

His voice rang with indignation. 'I've never had a mistress in my life—lots of one-night stands that I'm not proud of, but no mistress. I've never wanted to spend that much time with a woman.'

It was Valentina's turn to flush. She felt confused and didn't like the warm glow his words left in her gut. 'So... why did you...?' She trailed off and then tacked on, 'Look, if you felt that I was letting you down with my own clothes you could have just said something and I'd have gone shopping myself.'

Gio straightened up from the door and ran a hand through his hair, messing it up. '*Dio*. I didn't feel as if you were letting me down. Damn it, Valentina, you could have been dressed in a sack and still outshone every woman there. You'd mentioned that you hadn't had time to shop....'

The glow of warmth in Valentina's gut spread and she panicked when she recalled her earlier vulnerability, the temptation to put on one of the dresses, wanting to look beautiful for Gio. That suddenly galvanised her into movement and Valentina stalked into the bedroom and gathered all the dresses up, along with the shoes, underwear and jewellery, in her arms.

Uncaring of the fact that she was leaving a trail behind her, she was only intent on getting rid of Gio and this reminder of how fragile she was around him. She came back and dumped it on a chair near him, the red dress slithering to a silken mound on the floor.

Valentina was breathing far more heavily than that little trip had warranted. She crossed her arms again and looked at Gio, who caught her gaze with a suspiciously impassive expression.

'Look, I appreciate it, really. But I can buy my own clothes and I'll go shopping tomorrow.'

A little scared by Gio's lack of reaction Valentina blurted out, 'It's not as if you went to the trouble of getting them yourself....' She flushed when she thought of the exquisite underwear and had a sudden fantasy that Gio *had* looked at it and imagined her in it. That spurred her back into the bedroom and she returned holding out the typewritten note. She held it up like evidence at a trial. 'Look! Your assistant wrote this—you probably weren't even aware of what you were signing.'

Gio's arms were crossed now and he growled softly, 'Yes, I was, because *I* wrote that note. No one else. Just like I had the boutique send over a selection of dresses and I chose the ones I thought would suit you best.'

Valentina's hand dropped and the note fell from numb

fingers to the floor. *Dio*. He had picked it all out. He had looked at it. Had he imagined—? Her mind seized at the thought.

Heat suffused Valentina to have it confirmed that he had chosen it. Himself. Increasingly panicked now she crossed her arms and said, 'It doesn't matter. I just want you to go.'

'But it does matter,' he insisted softly, coming closer. 'You see, I don't like you thinking that I could be insensitive enough to order you something as intimate as underwear via my secretary. After all, how would she even know your size?'

Gio continued. 'I have severe dyslexia. It's a condition I've had to learn to live with all my life and thankfully there is now a plethora of software out there to help people with my condition. That note was dictated by me, into a very handy machine which then printed it off, whereupon I signed it with my customary signature of *G* because it's simply easier. And distinctive to anyone who knows me.'

Valentina's arms were crossed so tightly across her chest now she feared she might cut off the blood supply to her brain. Gio's mention of his dyslexia was throwing up memories of Mario sitting patiently beside him, laboriously working through homework assignments from Gio's expensive prep school. She'd forgotten. And didn't like the reminder, or the tender urges that came with it.

On jelly legs Valentina went to the door and opened it wide and stood back. 'Thank you for that explanation. I appreciate it. I'll return the dresses tomorrow and buy something suitable. I'd just like it if you left now. Please.'

But Gio didn't appear to be listening. He was pacing back and forth and then he stopped suddenly and turned to face her, something so carnal and stark on his face that her whole body went slowly on fire.

'The fact is that I did buy those dresses for a reason… and it wasn't because you weren't dressed appropriately. It was because I wanted to see you in them. I bought the underwear too, and I imagined how it would fit.…'

Valentina felt faint; her sweaty hand nearly slipped off the door handle. All she could feel was searing heat and all she could see was Gio.

He came towards her before she had time to react and pushed the door closed again behind her and locked it. Valentina was trapped against the door but had a curious inability or wish to move. She could only look up at him and ask redundantly, 'Why?'

Gio's arms were braced either side of her head. His whole body was caging her in. His scent, his proximity… Valentina couldn't move, couldn't think straight.

'Because of *this*.' And then Gio bent towards her and, without touching another part of her body, pressed his mouth to hers, and the world went on fire.

It felt like aeons later when Valentina surfaced from the kiss to look up into Gio's dark green-flecked eyes. Her lips felt swollen. His hand was on her waist and she was clinging to his shirt; it was bunched in her hands. She hadn't even been aware of doing that. She could see herself reflected in his pupils, a tiny figure, and suddenly she remembered the excoriating rejection of the other night, how she'd vowed to him and herself that she wouldn't let him touch her again. She'd just broken that promise with little or no persuasion.

Disgusted with herself she let go of Gio's shirt and pushed away from him, and tried to ignore the way the beat of her blood was calling her back to him like a magnet. When she felt able, she turned around and wrapped her arms around her body in an unconsciously protective gesture.

She looked at Gio with huge eyes. 'I can't do this with you. I won't do this with you. With anyone else but you.

'After all,' she reminded him bitterly, 'I'm still a virgin, Gio. I haven't managed to offload that burden yet.'

Fire and rage rushed through Gio with frightening force, at the *very thought*.... He ground out with an almost savage intensity, 'And you won't...with anyone else, except me.'

He came towards her and Valentina stepped back holding out an arm, as if that could stop him. Fires were racing all over her skin at the way he'd just sounded and the look of intent on his face. The magnitude of what could happen here if she let it. *And how much she wanted it*. Valentina had to fight it. She called up how it had felt when he'd handed her that robe and avoided her eyes. *I don't sleep with virgins*.

'Wait.' Her voice shook. 'How dare you suddenly decide that you've got any kind of right to make such a statement. You were very clear in your rejection the other evening.'

'I didn't want to reject you.' Gio's voice was rough and husky, weakening Valentina's resolve. 'Walking away was the hardest thing I've ever done but I did it because I knew if I'd taken you, you would have woken afterwards and despised me even more than you already do.'

Those words lanced her deep inside. She thought he'd rejected her because he just didn't want to sleep with her *enough*. She felt like an abject fraud because, if anything, she might have despised herself for being so weak, not him, but this was her only defence against Gio now. She tipped up her chin. 'And what makes now any different?'

'What makes it different is that I'm willing to risk your hatred because I want you too much. I'm not strong enough to stand back and watch some other man become your first lover.'

Valentina saw Gio's hands curled to fists and felt his very tangible passion. The thought of some other man touching her, kissing her, almost made bile rise from her gullet.

Without Valentina realising it, Gio had come closer. He reached out a hand now and cupped her jaw, his fingers trailing against her neck where she could feel her pulse beating almost out of control.

He just said, 'You want me…you can't deny it, not here and now.'

'I…' she croaked and stopped, feeling seriously out of her depth. She couldn't deny it. To deny it would be to utter the worst of falsehoods. Gio knew it. She knew it.

And in that moment she also knew that she was tacitly acquiescing because she had no choice. This had been building and building between them from the moment she'd seen him at the wedding just weeks before. *And a long time before that*, a small rogue voice insisted.

Gio smiled and it was unbearably bleak. 'I'm giving you full permission to despise me all you want in the aftermath, Valentina, because I know you will. At least this way there can be total honesty between us. It's physical, that's *all*.'

His acceptance of her antipathy made something ache inside Valentina, but the promise of no emotions also freed something. She knew she could never love someone and risk losing them again, the way she'd lost Mario. Something pure and innocent inside her had been lost for ever that night. The grief was too deep, too raw. Gio was too inextricably bound up with pain for her, and guilt. The guilt of the shameful secret she was still too cowardly to acknowledge.

The shadow of Mario's death was too long. But she wanted him. She'd never connected with another man on such a visceral, physical level. This would burn out, it had to. Intensity like this couldn't last....

As if reading her thoughts, Gio said, 'This will burn out, and when it does...we'll move on.'

We'll move on. Valentina wondered if they really could move on, find some kind of closure. For a long moment nothing was said. Valentina looked into Gio's eyes until she felt as if she were drowning. And then she felt some great resistance she'd been clinging on to dissolve within her. She couldn't fight this.

She put her hand over his on her jaw and turned her face so that she could press a kiss to his palm. She closed her eyes but she could feel the tremor that went through his body, or was it hers? She couldn't tell.

Gio moved closer to her, putting a hand to the small of her back, and tugged her closer. Valentina sent up a fervent prayer that they could move on from this, because she didn't have the strength to stop now. And as his mouth met hers and she melted into him and his kiss, it felt so *right*.

Gio was trying to curb the rush of desire sending his brain into a fiery orbit. Valentina felt so unutterably good in his arms. Soft and pliant and curvy. Her breasts were pressed against his chest and he could feel the thrust of hard nipples. Letting his hand drop he found the sweet curve of her bottom and cupped it, softly at first and then harder when he felt the instinctive sway of her hips towards him.

Victory was heady and he was rapidly getting lost in the nectar of the sweetest kiss. As sweet as it was though, he wanted more; he wanted harder, darker. He wanted to be inside her, and he had to be careful. She was innocent. Exerting extreme self-control Gio managed to somehow break the connection and pull back, almost groaning when he saw how long it took for Valentina to open heavy-lidded eyes, their dark depths even darker, pupils huge. Her lips dark red and swollen.

'Let's take this slow...OK?'

Valentina sucked in a breath, trying to force oxygen to her short-circuiting brain. That had just been a kiss and a relatively chaste one and already she felt as if she were burning up from the inside out.

Before she could articulate anything that might sound vaguely coherent Gio was taking her by the hand and leading her into the bedroom. He pushed her back gently towards the bed and she collapsed onto the edge to find him at her feet, those big capable hands moving up her legs and under the dress.

He looked up at her for a second. *Lord.* Valentina could feel her lower belly muscles clench hard. She couldn't speak, could only watch as Gio's eyes went back to her legs and watch how they cupped behind her knees before inching ever higher, pushing her dress up inexorably until her legs were bared.

Gio's cheeks were flushed and Valentina felt the warmth of his calloused palms move up until they cupped her buttocks intimately. She gasped. He was right between her legs now, pushing them apart. She half collapsed back onto the bed, her elbows the only thing holding her up.

Gio looked up at her and said throatily, 'Trust me?'

Valentina bit her lip and after a heated moment nodded her head. Without taking his eyes off hers Valentina could feel him lift her gently so that he could push her dress all the way up; now her entire lower body was exposed to him. For a fleeting second she wished ardently that she *was* wearing one of the impossibly delicate lace panties and not her very plain black ones.

But she soon forgot about that when she felt Gio's hands

find her panties and slowly start to move them down and
Valentina felt herself lifting her hips ever so slightly to
help. Somewhere she was aware of a shocked part of herself wondering how on earth she was letting this happen.
With this man? When only minutes ago she'd been trying to throw him out of this room. But like a coward she
blocked it out; this growing, pulling desire in her body
was too strong.

Gio pulled Valentina's panties off and threw them somewhere on the ground; now she was exposed to him completely, her dress bunched up over her waist. They seemed
to have passed go and gone straight to level one hundred
but all Valentina could see was the way Gio was looking
at her with such awe and reverence, his big hands now on
her thighs, spreading her for him.

He bent and pressed kisses along her sensitive inner
thighs and she could feel the bristle of his stubble. It en-
flamed her nerve endings and she squirmed against his
mouth, only to have his hands tighten on her, silently ordering her to be still.

His mouth was getting higher and higher, rising inexorably to the apex of her legs where she felt so hot and yet
indecently damp. When his breath feathered there Valentina's elbows gave out and she collapsed onto the bed,
just as Gio's mouth found her and she felt his tongue touch
her moist cleft.

She had to put a fist to her mouth and bite down hard
against the pleasure he was now wreaking on her body
with such shocking intimacy. He was licking her, tasting her and ruthlessly pushing those legs apart when they
wanted to close against this exquisite invasion.

And then she felt his tongue opening her up to him, exploring and stabbing deep inside, tasting her very essence.
Valentina felt faint. A finger joined his tongue, pushing

and stretching. She could feel her hips moving against his mouth, seeking more, a deeper penetration. She felt so stretched and yet unfulfilled and wanted more. A tight feeling was coiling deep inside her, getting tighter and tighter, making her move even more restlessly.

Then she felt two fingers, pushing deeper, and his tongue found and circled her clitoris with ruthless sucking intensity until Valentina broke free of the building tension to soar high to a place she'd ever seen before. Waves of pleasure more intense than she could have ever imagined broke through her and over her. It was so stupendous she couldn't even cry out, absorbing it in shocked silence, biting into her fist even harder in a bid to contain what she felt.

As she floated back down into some sense of reality Valentina became aware that she was still throbbing in spasms, deep inside her. Her fist fell from her mouth, too heavy to hold up any more. Gio's hands were gone and she looked up languorously to see him rise up like some kind of avenging God to rip open his shirt to reveal that magnificent chest. His eyes burnt into hers, and his hands went to his trousers, making quick work of his belt, buttons and zip.

Valentina couldn't even lift her head, it felt so heavy. She was aware of being displayed wantonly towards him but couldn't drum up a sense of shame. Not after what she'd just experienced. She'd never known it could be like that....

'I want to see you,' Gio muttered thickly, finding her hands and pulling her gently upwards. Valentina sat up and felt light-headed. Gio was pulling her to her feet and found her zip, yanking it down, and taking her dress with it so that it dropped at her feet with a soft swishing sound. Now she stood before him in nothing but her own plain bra and Gio's dark eyes were molten as they looked her up and down.

To her surprise, Valentina could feel some of the delicious lethargy move and shift, dissipate, so that she was being infected by a rising sense of tension again. It coiled deep inside her. Gio was naked and she looked down to see his erection thrusting towards her. Instinctively she reached for him, wanting to touch him, and wrapped a hand around his thick impressive length.

He breathed deep and his hands tightened on her arms where they'd gone to steady her a moment ago. Valentina was fascinated by the feel of him under her hand; he was like steel encased in velvet, infinitely strong and hard and yet so vulnerable. She looked up and her hand stopped when she saw the stark and almost feral need imprinted on his face. She gulped.

Gently he took her hand off him and said, 'I don't know how long I can last if you touch me like that. And I need to last—this is your first time....'

Valentina's heart seemed to miss a beat. Her first time, here with this man. The reality suddenly hit her, along with the very fervent assertion that she didn't want to be anywhere else. That threw up all sorts of emotional contradictions within her and to drive them down where she didn't have to analyse them Valentina stepped up to Gio and put her hands on his face.

'Gio...' Her voice was husky and rough. 'Make love to me.'

Her words hung in the desire-saturated air for a long moment and then Gio wrapped his arms around her and pulled her into him, driving his mouth down onto hers and kissing her so thoroughly she felt dizzy with need.

Valentina was barely aware of Gio undoing her bra so that it dropped to the floor between them. She only came back to her senses when she felt herself being lowered back onto the bed and looked up to see Gio hover over her on two hands, huge and dark and devastating. Shoulders broad, chest wide, hips narrow and lean. And lower, where the trail of very masculine hair ended, jutted his arousal. Valentina's eyes widened. She could see a pearlescent bead of moisture at the tip of his erection and her lower body clenched in instinctive response to such a display of male virility.

Gio started to press his mouth in a series of hot kisses all the way up from her belly to her ribs. Valentina held her breath. After an achingly long moment she felt him stretch out beside her on the bed and he cupped one breast, before his breath feathered over the distended tingling tip and he drew it into his mouth. The sheer sensation of that torturous delicious tugging sucking heat made Valentina's hips buck off the bed, her feet desperately searching for anything to dig into.

When Gio's mouth went to her other breast Valentina was nearly sobbing aloud from the sheer pleasure. She could feel heat gather between her legs, and as if guided there by her mind, Gio's free hand gently pushed her thighs apart, as he sought access.

Valentina was too incoherent to stop him. With skilful precision, Gio parted her thighs wider and his fingers found the aching core of her body, fingers stroking and spreading her moist arousal. Valentina's hands clutched at Gio's shoulders, fingers digging deep into satin skin, dewed with sweat. Their combined scent, musky and tart with desire, only served to make her feel even hotter.

Gio took his mouth off Valentina's breast and moved up to her mouth. She met him blindly, tongues lashing together as need mounted. She could feel a tremor run through Gio's body beside her and had a fleeting sense of

just how much he was holding back. As his tongue delved
deep into her mouth, his fingers thrust inside her, deeply
intimate. It was so sudden and yet shockingly arousing that
Valentina gasped against his mouth. Tiny waves and tremors of another incipient orgasm started up and she drew
back to look up at Gio in wonder. His eyes were black,
molten. No more green flecks.

His fingers slowly started to move in and out. Valentina could feel herself being stretched and on the periph-
ery of the mounting excitement and pleasure was the slight
tinge of pain.

'I want to prepare you…make sure you're ready for me.'

At that moment Valentina felt Gio's arousal, heavy
against her hip. Long and thick and hard. She sucked in a
breath as his words sank in. 'Oh…'

'Yes…' He smiled wryly. 'Oh…'

As Gio's fingers picked up pace though, Valentina
quickly stopped being able to rationalise anything. Her
hands clutched at his shoulders again and her head went
back, hips raising of their own accord. She moved them
restlessly, seeking something…more.

'Gio…' she whispered brokenly. She felt something
give inside her. It was a fleeting moment of sharp pain
and Gio pulled his hand away. Valentina looked at him,
blinking. Her body was still crying out for his touch, despite the pain.

'Gio?'

Gio moved his body so that he hovered over her now,
pushing her legs apart with his hips. She could feel the
heavy length of him brushing against her sex. He took
himself in his hand and Valentina looked down to see that
he'd sheathed himself with protection with no idea of when
or where he'd had the wherewithal to do it.

He was running the thick head of his penis along where

she felt drenched with desire. So much that it embarrassed her. With that realisation she turned her head to the side, suddenly overwhelmed.

She felt him still and a hand come to her chin, turning her back. His face was etched with desire but also something else that made her quiver: *concern*.

'Valentina?'

She took refuge from the tender feeling his concern aroused by focusing on the needs of her physical body. 'I want you...'

The concern faded from Gio's face and a stark primality took over. She could feel him position himself, feel his fingers on himself and on her as he slowly fed himself into her, inch by thick inch. The initial sensation was overpowering. Valentina sucked in a breath at the intrusion. This was so much more devastating than his fingers. But even as she thought that, her body seemed to recognise something she didn't, or trust something she didn't, and she could feel her muscles opening, admitting entrance.

With a guttural groan Gio took his hand away and rested on both hands over her body. With a hoarse calling out of her name, he thrust deep and hard and sheathed himself in her completely.

Valentina's eyes opened wide and her chest expanded with the breath she'd drawn in. Her hands were on his biceps where she could feel them quiver under her fingers. He was shaking, or she was shaking; she wasn't sure which.

She felt impossibly full and impaled, invaded. Gio was looking down at her, that concern edging back. 'OK?'

Valentina jerkily nodded her head. 'Please...Gio...'

Slowly he started to move, out...and then back in. His movements within her were so exquisite, bordering between pain and pleasure, that Valentina could only breathe in short gasps, struggling to hang on to whatever control she still had. She felt as if she was in danger of exploding into a million fragments with each long slide of Gio's body back into hers. And with each stroke, the pain faded to be replaced and eclipsed by pleasure.

Without even realising what she was doing, her feet were digging into the bed beside Gio's hips; her own were moving restlessly. As if sensing her inner turmoil over all this newness, Gio bent and pressed a kiss to her mouth, tongue stroking along hers for a long moment, soothing but also inciting.

'Wrap your legs around me,' he whispered in her ear, 'and I'll help you to fly.'

She could feel him find her leg and lift it up over one hip and blindly she lifted her other leg, wrapping both legs around those lean hips, ankles crossed just above his buttocks. He sank even deeper within her and their moans mingled. Valentina could feel his chest hairs scrape her sensitised breasts, making her arch upwards, seeking that contact again.

Gio's movements became more urgent. He was thrusting so hard and so deep now that Valentina saw stars. And then without any warning at all, her entire body clenched tight before exploding into a million pieces. Valentina gasped, head back, bucking uncontrollably against Gio as he pounded into her, his own release finally stilling that huge body just as he touched the very core of her.

In the aftermath Valentina's brain couldn't wrap itself around the magnitude of what had just happened. The pain mixed with a pleasure more intense than she'd ever experienced. She was vaguely aware of Gio pulling free of her body and disappearing for a moment before returning. She was vaguely aware of him lifting her body so that her head touched a pillow. He drew a thin cover over her body. When he tucked himself around her, she found that she was instinctively twining her legs around his, holding him to her tightly.

He lifted an arm and she felt his fingers smoothing damp strands of hair from her face. She opened sleepy eyes and caught a glimpse of a mark on the inside of his upper left arm. In the dim light she hadn't noticed it before. Without thinking Valentina reached up to trace what looked like black marks etched into his skin. A tattoo of some sort. She frowned. 'What's this?'

Gio's fingers in her hair stilled and she felt him tense. After a long moment he drew his arm back from her questing fingers and just said, 'It's nothing…rest now.'

He shifted his body so that Valentina was curled into his side, and with her cheek resting on his chest over where his heart beat steadily, she found herself slipping down into a dark dreamless place. She would think about those marks…later. She would think about it all.

As the dawn light filtered into Valentina's room, bathing everything in a pinky gold, Gio sat in a chair in the corner of her room. He'd pulled on his trousers, leaving them open, and just watched the woman who lay sleeping in the bed.

She was on her front, the sheet provocatively resting just over her buttocks, revealing the long smooth curve of her back. One arm was curled up to her chest where he could just make out the swell of her breast. His body tightened predictably and Gio grimaced at the response.

Her other arm was flung out by her head and her cheek rested on the pillow, long black lashes casting a shadow on flushed cheeks. Still flushed. He remembered how it had felt to sink into her velvet hot embrace, how tight she'd been at first…. His own body tightened even more and Gio gave up castigating himself for such a helpless response.

It had been the hardest thing in the world to extricate himself from Valentina's embrace but a part of him hadn't relished the prospect of her expression when she woke to find herself curled around him so comprehensively. And another part of him had needed to get some space…to try and rationalise the sheer scale of what had just happened.

Gio had never experienced sex like that…so intense and primal. His face grew stark—admittedly, many of his previous experiences were a blur from those two hellish years. But even before that…it had never been like this. He'd never lost control, lost himself so completely. Mario had used to tease him mercilessly: *You won't be able to cut yourself off forever, Gio. One day you'll meet someone who won't let you stay so aloof….*

The truth was, Gio had envied the ease with which Mario had fallen in and out of love. Gio just hadn't had that capacity. Emotions for him were a dark and dangerous place to explore. Once, when he'd been tiny, he'd gone to his father with something he'd made, desperate to try and get his attention, acutely aware of how his older brothers seemed to effortlessly get and hold their father's attention in a way he couldn't.

Gio had stood in front of his father holding out the model airplane he'd spent hours working on. He could remember that all he'd wanted to say was, *I made this for you.* But under his father's arctic judgemental glare the words just wouldn't come out.

His father had snapped at him, irritated at this hesitance, and Gio could remember how his hands had trembled. The less he'd been able to speak, the more angry his father had become until he'd ripped the airplane out of Gio's hands, thrown it to the ground and stamped on it.

A lot of his father's vile words from that day were forgotten, but not the acrid sense of betrayal and hurt. Or the way his mother had shrank into the shadows, unable to stand up for her youngest son, too scared of directing that wrath towards her when she was so desperately trying to get back into her husband's favour.

He'd learnt to draw inwards that day, to protect himself.

A movement from the bed made Gio focus on Valentina again. He welcomed the distraction. She was uncurling her arm from her side and Gio could see the swell of her plump breast. With fire igniting in his veins again he stood up and went over, sitting beside her on the edge of the bed.

Slowly she opened her eyes. He saw her try to focus, to assimilate the information her body was undoubtedly giving her. And then she saw him. Those amber feline eyes widened, the flush on her cheeks deepened. Gio's chest constricted when he could see the myriad questions about to come out of her mouth.

Without thinking he put a finger to her lips, their softness making him ache. 'Shh…don't think…don't say anything…just let it be….'

Gio watched her wary response, and then as if some inner turmoil had been resolved she nodded imperceptibly. He took his finger away and said throatily, 'How do you feel? Are you sore?'

Even as he watched he could see the glowing embers of desire in her eyes, and his arousal soared. Looking endearingly shy now, she just shook her head against the pillow.

'Good,' Gio said and bent down to press a kiss to her mouth. She turned onto her back, opening up her body to him again and Gio fell back into the glorious blaze once more.

CHAPTER EIGHT

Valentina was in deeply unchartered waters. She was standing in her shower with her eyes closed and Gio was massaging shampoo into her hair. She felt like purring. She also felt like turning around and pushing him up against the wall and kissing him all over. She could feel his erection brush against her buttocks and had to put her hands out to touch the tiles, afraid she'd fall down in a heap at his feet under the teeming hot spray.

She felt him turn her around and kept her eyes closed, too scared to look and see that gorgeous physique up close. That physique that had taken her to heaven and back more times than she could remember during the previous night and then again that morning. She'd never known the human body was capable of such pleasure, of such base carnal desires. Or that those desires could be felt, and *met*.

But more than all of that, she was too scared to open her eyes and look into Gio's. To see the same expression she'd seen in them this morning when she'd woken to find him looking at her so intently, as if he could see all the way into her soul, where she hid her deepest secrets.

But she couldn't avoid it. Not when Gio pronounced her clean and tipped her chin up with a finger. With the utmost reluctance she opened her eyes and looked up. Gio had stopped the water but they were still surrounded by steamy warm air, like a sensual cocoon. Lazily he put his arm out, hand touching the wall behind her. It was then that Valentina noticed the marks again, on his arm. The tattoo.

He saw where her gaze had gone and in an instant the atmosphere went from hot and sultry to cool as ice. He quickly took down his arm again, reaching out for towels. So fast that her head span, Gio had manoeuvred her out of the shower and was wrapping her in a huge soft towel and hitching one around his own hips.

Curiosity well and truly stoked now, Valentina followed Gio into the bedroom. He'd lifted the towel off his hips and was roughly rubbing his hair before running it over the rest of his body in a very perfunctory manner, clearly doing his utmost to get out of her room quickly. Valentina tried desperately not to let his naked back and those firmly sculpted buttocks distract her. Just looking at his powerfully muscled thighs made her think of how potently masculine he'd felt between her legs.

She hitched her own towel under her arms sarong-style and ignored the fact that she was dripping water all over the floor. She went over and stood in front of a very naked and damp Gio. She crossed her arms against the betraying rush of heat to her groin.

'What are those marks?'

Gio scowled and for a second looked endearingly young. Oozing reluctance he wrapped his towel around his hips and crossed his own arms, effectively hiding the tattoo in question.

Growing exasperated now Valentina reached out and pulled at his arms, making him loosen them, and then she held his left arm up, so that she could see the tattoo clearly. 'Why on earth don't you want to talk about this? It's just a tattoo....'

Saying something finally, Gio bit out, 'Exactly, it's nothing.'

He tried to pull his arm back but Valentina held on tenaciously, inspecting the uniform black ink marks. Out loud she said, 'They look like roman numerals…some kind of a date? Four…five…'

She could read the first part, but the last piece eluded her—her knowledge of roman numerals only went up to about ten but this was clearly a much larger number, and as she realised this, she also realised the significance of *four* and *five*. Mario had died on the fourth of May.…

Valentina dropped Gio's arm and looked up at him. She could feel the blood draining southwards. Gio cursed under his breath and guided her to the bed to sit down on the edge. He stood in front of her and admitted with stark reluctance, 'It's the date Mario died.'

Valentina's belly clenched hard. Every line of Gio's body was screaming at her to *stay out of this*.

'But…' She tried to formulate words, to understand. 'Why?'

Gio cursed again and turned away, pacing impatiently to the window, presenting her with his rigid back. Without turning around he said bleakly, 'I needed to mark the date…when Mario's life ended, and mine.'

Before, Valentina knew she would have jumped down his throat and reminded him that his life hadn't ended. But after what he'd told her of his experiences she had to concede that it *had* ended on some level.

After the intimacies of the previous night it was very hard to call up the rage she'd clung to for so long. *This is what she'd been afraid of.*

The thought of him asking some stranger to carve an indelible mark into his skin made her feel unaccountably emotional. Before she knew what she was doing she'd stood up and went over to Gio. She inserted herself between him and the window, his jaw was as rigid as the rest of him and he looked at her warily.

Dropping her gaze to his arms, she once again undid them from where they were crossed so tightly. She took his marked arm and held it out again, turned up so she could see the tattoo. With her finger she traced the lines, feeling the indentation in his skin, marked for ever with this brand of the date her brother had died.

His guilt reached out to envelop her in that moment and it was so suffocating that she stepped back, letting his arm drop heavily. Panic prickled in her belly. For one awful second she'd wanted to place her mouth over that tattoo, to kiss Gio there, to assuage his pain…and that was a revelation she wasn't ready for.

Feeling rigid all over, the previous night all but forgotten in her bid to put some space between herself and his man, Valentina stepped back and said, 'I should get ready for work.'

She went into the bathroom and turned the lock in the door. And then she rested her back against the door. She half expected to hear Gio demand autocratically that she open up and remembered his own reluctance to admit what the tattoo was. But nothing happened.

It was only when she heard her main apartment door open and close and she knew that Gio had left that she allowed herself to sink to the floor and silent tears leaked from her eyes.

She wasn't even sure what she was crying for…but for once it wasn't grief for Mario; it was for something much deeper and more ambiguous. Allowing herself that glimpse of Gio's pain and guilt had shaken her to her very core. And deep down, in that dark and secret place within her, the shameful truth she'd harboured for seven years was rising back to the surface.

Valentina was aware that if she were to acknowledge it now, it would blast apart everything that had been holding her together since Mario had died…and if she didn't have that, who was she?

As Gio walked away from Valentina's accommodation his gut churned. *The tattoo.* Of course she'd noticed the tattoo. He'd been drunk when he'd got it, full of bile and self-recrimination. Guilt. A perverse part of him had liked the thought of being marked for ever, so he could never forget. As if that were possible.

For a crazy second back there, he'd almost fancied that Valentina had been moved enough by the tattoo that she'd… She'd *what*? a voice mocked him bitterly. That she'd understood something of his experience? That she possibly didn't hate him as much as he thought she did?

His mouth firmed. She would never forgive him. And she certainly wasn't interested in absolving him.

Gio resolutely pushed tender emotional roots back down into the murky darkness of his damaged soul and vowed that if the physical was all he was going to get with Valentina, then he would take it. And let her walk away when she'd had enough. Even though the thought of that made him want to smash his fist through the nearest solid object.

'Mini doughnuts to go with mini coffees for dessert…and the sweet fig starter…truly inspired…'

Valentina smiled weakly and cursed herself inwardly. This was what she'd been waiting for, an opportunity to showcase her skills in front of the very people who could take her forward with her career and yet she couldn't concentrate. She was too keyed up, her whole body quivering because she knew Gio was just feet away in the crowded throng. Guests were finishing lunch in the VIP marquee and moving back outside for the biggest race of the three days.

Valentina gave up trying to focus on what the guests were saying to her and murmured her thanks and excuses, cursing herself again that she was so distracted. She turned to head back out to the main tent to make sure that everything was set up for the inevitable celebrations after the race and ran straight into a wall of steel.

Gio.

She looked up. His hands were on her arms and her legs felt like jelly. His gaze raked her up and down and dimly she realised that he'd shaved since the morning. He looked…edible. Her insides melted. She thought of the tattoo and her heart clenched.

'OK?'

It took a second for his question to register. She was too caught up in her reaction to him. Jerkily she nodded her head and then she realised that he was standing with another couple. The man was tall, as tall as Gio. There was a startling resemblance even though Valentina knew it wasn't one of his brothers. A woman stood beside the man, his hand in a proprietorial hold on her arm, much the same way Gio now held Valentina's arm. It was only then that she became aware of the crackling tension between the men.

In that instance some flicker of affinity passed between the women, even though Valentina had never seen her before. She was beautiful, with long straight brown hair and stunning blue eyes.

'Angelo, I'd like you to meet Valentina Ferranti, the woman who has been in charge of catering for this year's Corretti Cup.'

The man smiled and Valentina felt Gio's hand tighten on her fractionally. He was stupendously handsome, even though he did nothing for Valentina. He put out a hand and said urbanely, 'Nice to meet you. I'm Gio's illegitimate cousin. I'm also betting against his horse today and I expect to win.'

Before Valentina could respond Gio was biting out, 'She's got nothing to do with our pathetic family dramas.'

Valentina took Angelo's hand and felt something inexplicably primal rise up within her. She smiled sweetly. 'We'll be serving Prosecco and elderflower cocktails after the race to help you drown your sorrows when you lose to Gio's horse.'

Angelo kept ahold of her hand and after a long moment he looked from Valentina to Gio and said with steel in his voice, 'We'll see.'

Shocked at that protective surge she'd felt to defend Gio, Valentina took her hand back and jerked her arm out of Gio's hold. Focusing on no one in particular she muttered something about needing to check something and left the tent.

Thankfully things were gearing up for the big race so Valentina knew that Gio would be busy and unlikely to come after her and she needed some space. She couldn't keep avoiding her own conscience after last night and that morning.

She found a secluded spot hidden away from everything and leant against the railing of a nearby paddock, resting her forehead on her hands. Her insides felt as if they were cramping. Her breath was choppy. She shouldn't have slept with Gio…and yet, Valentina had enough honesty to admit that if she went back in time, was confronted with Gio all over again…no force on earth could have induced her to resist.

But the tattoo…what he'd been through after Mario's death—it all whirled sickeningly in her head now.

'What is it? What's wrong?'

Valentina was being pulled up from the railing, her heart slamming to a halt before she even realised that Gio had followed her. Sudden anger at this invasion of privacy when she felt so vulnerable made her lash out. 'Nothing is wrong, Gio, apart from the fact that I despise myself for being so weak!'

Every line in Gio's face stood out in stark relief. 'I told you last night, Valentina. I give you full permission to despise *me*. And believe me, I have every intention of making you despise me over and over again.'

He reached out with two hands and pulled her into him before she could take a breath and then his mouth was fusing to hers. The kiss was desperate and brutal but electrifying. Anger and pain and remorse all clawed up within Valentina seeking release. Desperately she clutched at his head, holding him to her, allowing no escape. Teeth bit and drew blood before Gio stopped, breathing harshly, his forehead resting on Valentina's. She was dizzy with the sudden overwhelming surge of need mixed with adrenalin.

'Hate *me*, Valentina…not yourself. This thing…it's out of our control.'

Gio stood up straight and pulled back even though it was the hardest thing in the world. Valentina's smooth top knot was coming undone. Her mouth was red and swollen, her chest rising up and down as she tried to regain her breath. A few buttons had opened on her white shirt, giving him a tantalising glimpse of her lacy bra and cleavage. And Gio knew he had to get out of there now or he'd take her on the ground like an animal.

He turned and walked away before he did anything else

and realised that, by the time this insanity was over between them, he'd be torn apart completely.

Valentina looked after Gio, struck dumb by his curt, *Hate
me, Valentina*. Tears pricked her eyes. She wanted to call
out; she wanted to make him stop. She wanted to say *sorry*.
But like a coward, she didn't. The truth sat heavily in her
belly. She didn't despise herself for being weak…she despised herself for feeling so many disturbing emotions
for this man and for not having the courage to own up to
them, or analyse them.

Distaste flickered across Gio's face. The gala auction had
been under way for some time now and the huge sums of
money were becoming more outrageous as people helped
themselves to increasing quantities of alcohol.

    Not so long ago he had been one of those people, fling-
ing huge sums of money into the ether in some desperate
bid to seek solace.

    His cousin Angelo had come to him before leaving with
his date and had shook Gio's hand in recognition of the
fact that he had indeed lost to Gio's far superior horse in
the race. But to Gio's surprise, while their conversation
was sharp and cool, he'd felt a burgeoning respect for the
man and they'd parted on more than civil note. He found
himself slightly amazed when his usual reaction to anyone
in his family was to walk quickly in the other direction.

    A flash of dark red caught Gio's eye then and he looked,
his gaze stopping and fixing on Valentina where she'd
just arrived into the VIP tent. *She was wearing one of the
dresses.* The knowledge sent something very primal into
his blood.

    She'd somehow managed to avoid him all evening—al-
ways flitting to and fro on the opposite side of wherever

he was, and too surrounded by people eager to share in his Corretti Cup race success Gio had been trapped. Until now. His whole body tingled and arousal was fierce and immediate. He'd had a vision of her in this dress as soon as he'd seen it but the reality was far more stupendous.

Her hair was up, in a slightly messy chignon, exposing her long delicate neck. Her shoulders were bare and pale. Her breasts swelled against the heart-shaped neckline of the dress and tight bodice before it fell to the floor in a swathe of silk and chiffon.

She wore no jewellery, and a minimum of make-up. And she was more beautiful than any other woman there. A fact which seemed to have impacted on not only him. Gio saw a lurching movement towards her and recognised the French playboy.

Gio was moving before he'd even realised his intention and he pushed down the memory of her words earlier, how deeply they'd cut into him. He'd followed her outside after their exchange with Angelo because he'd been stunned at how she'd defended him. He should have realised that it had meant nothing.

The hurt from earlier solidified in his belly and he blocked it out, welcoming the heat in his blood. This was all he wanted, this oblivion she could give him. And hate herself for, a small voice reminded him. He was too weak to turn back now and his vision went red when he saw his erstwhile friend reach Valentina and clamp a hand around her arm.

Valentina had just arrived back into the VIP tent. Instinctively she found herself searching out a familiar tall and broad figure when her eyes adjusted to the artfully lit space. When she didn't see him immediately she blocked out the way her belly hollowed out. She felt very exposed, as if she was sending Gio some silent message because after a long intense internal struggle earlier, she'd finally put on one of the dresses Gio had bought for her.

It, and the matching underwear, felt exactly as decadent as she'd feared it would, along with the very scary sense of being on tenterhooks all evening, waiting to see Gio and his reaction. Before she could look further though, her arm was taken in a harsh grip.

She looked up, surprised, into the arrogant features of the French playboy who had been trying to chat her up the other night. She could see in an instant that he was inebriated. His already harsh grip tightened and immediately Valentina recoiled back, and tried to free herself but he hung on.

'Please let me go, Monsieur Lagarde.' She tried to keep her voice calm and reasonable over the sound of the crowd and the auctioneer.

'Oh, please…' he slurred. 'Surely we can be on first name terms, *non*? Call me Pierre….'

Valentina struggled again to free her arm, feeling a sliver of trepidation snake down her spine when she realised that he'd somehow manoeuvred them so that they were hidden from view behind a tall plant.

'You are so beautiful….'

He had both her arms in his hands now and Valentina felt panic claw upwards. He was huge, looming over her with his huge bulk. And then just as suddenly as the panic had risen, he was being lifted away from her as if by some magical force, his hands gone from her arms, making her stumble forward slightly.

He was replaced by a grim-looking Gio and all Valentina could see of Pierre was two of the discreet security men escorting him outside.

Gio cursed and came closer. 'He's bruised your arms.'

Valentina looked down stupidly and saw the red marks of his fingers. It was only then that she realised how scared she'd been for a few seconds. She looked up at Gio, aghast at the helpless emotion rising up within her, and knew shamefully that it had more to do with the man in front of her than what had just happened. She blinked rapidly to keep it back, but failed miserably.

Gio cursed again and she was being enveloped in his arms. Valentina felt faint with relief and how good it felt to have him hold her. Guilt compounded her as she soaked in his strength when she thought of what she'd said earlier.

She pulled back within his arms and looked up, words trembling on her lips. But once again Gio just put a finger to her mouth, silencing her. He shook his head. 'Don't say it.'

Valentina swallowed and spoke against his finger. 'But you don't know what I'm going to say.'

'I don't need to hear it, all I need is you.'

Valentina knew that if she was to pull free of Gio now, step back and say she didn't want him, he would let her go. He might not want to, but he would. It was etched into every tightly held muscle in his body.

Valentina knew there were a million and one reasons why she should take this opportunity to walk away. There was too much between them, too much that was tangled and dark and unspoken. But all she could feel was *him*. That dark seductive energy winding around her, binding her to him in some silent pact.

His assurance that she could do this and hate him for it made her feel riven with guilt…but she couldn't walk away. Just as she couldn't stop breathing.

But if she did this she also had to stop lashing out and blaming him. She had to take responsibility for her actions and hope that, soon, this temporary madness would cease and she could get on with her life. Even though right at that moment the thought of a life without Gio in it was inconceivable.

Valentina knew that if she tried to articulate any of this to Gio he'd just stop her. So she said, 'Can we just leave? Now?'

Valentina felt the faint tremor that ran through Gio's body and knew that he'd been as aware as her of how significant this moment was.

'Of course.'

His arms dropped and he stepped back, taking her hand. Valentina bit her lip and stopped him, suddenly aware of their surroundings. 'But…don't you have to stay? For the end of the auction?'

Gio just looked at her and flashed a sudden smile, making her breath stop momentarily. When he smiled like that he reminded her so much of *before*.

'I can delegate. Anyway, I don't think too many people here will be in any fit state to recall if I'm here or not at the end…and your work is done?'

Valentina nodded. Her staff were only concerned now with topping up glasses and the clear-up. It was over. She'd weathered her first bona fide exclusive event. As if reading her mind and sensing her relief Gio came close again and cupped her jaw before settling a sweet kiss on her mouth. He drew back. 'I meant to say thank you, you did a formidable job. I thought you'd appreciate knowing that my aunt Carmela nearly choked on her starter when she saw you directing proceedings earlier.'

Valentina melted inside at his words and couldn't help smiling too. She'd studiously ignored the frosty glares from the older woman but had been human enough to relish the second chance Gio had given her. Not only that, she'd been inundated with enquiries as to her availability for future events.

Gio was pulling her out from their secluded spot and Valentina tugged his hand again. 'Gio…'

He looked at her and she saw the fleeting trepidation on his face.

'I just wanted to say thank you…for the opportunity.'

'My pleasure…' He touched her jaw with a finger, leaving a trail of tingling fire in its wake, and said throatily, 'And it will be…'

Blazing heat seemed to consume Valentina like a flash fire. Both her hands were around Gio's where he held hers in a bid to stay upright as he all but pulled her from the tent. He stopped only momentarily to have words with one of his assistants and then he was striding out into the warm night air.

When she could see that Gio was heading in the direction of her rooms she found that she wanted to get away from here completely. She stopped in her tracks so Gio had to stop too. He looked back at her and the stark impatience on his face nearly made her change her mind. But she said, 'Not here…somewhere else.'

Gio frowned down at her. A wary light dawned in his eye. 'My *castello* is close…'

Where Mario died… Valentina waited for the inevitable pain to lance her but it didn't come. It felt right to want to go there and she couldn't explain it, but bizarrely it felt like a link to the past, a positive link.

'Your *castello*…yes.'

'Are you sure?'

Valentina nodded, impatience firing her own blood now. Abruptly Gio turned in his tracks and Valentina followed him to the private staff car park. He was unlocking his sports car but Valentina saw the huge monster of a mo-torbike beside it. She asked impetuously, 'Is that yours?'

Gio followed her look from where he was undoing his bow tie with long fingers. 'Yes, it's mine.'

His hand stilled. 'Why? Do you want to go on that in-stead?'

Valentina had a vivid memory of seeing Gio pull up outside her parents' humble home shortly after he'd come back from Europe. In jeans and a white T-shirt. No helmet.

She looked at him. 'Can we?'

Gio shrugged lightly. 'Sure…' He closed the car door and went to the bike, dislodging it from its parked posi-tion. With lithe grace he swung his leg over the pillion and settled into the main seat, his thighs straining against his trousers.

Looking back at Valentina he held out a hand. 'Hold on to me and step up onto the side and swing your leg over.'

Valentina bent down and slipped off her high-heeled sandals and hitched up her dress between her legs. Infec-tious excitement flared in her belly. Holding her shoes and dress in one hand, she balanced on Gio's shoulder with the other and felt his hand steady her, on her waist.

And then she was on the bike, nestled so snugly behind him that she could feel the indentation of his hard buttocks between her legs. A warm heat flooded through her. Gio was facing away from her again and then twisted back, holding out a helmet.

Valentina looked at it and then at him. 'Do I have to?'

'Yes,' he said firmly. 'If you want to go on this bike with me.'

Looking mildly amused at her mutinous expression Gio carefully put the helmet on her head and secured the strap before attending to himself.

Then he said over his shoulder, 'Put your hands around my waist and hold on.'

Valentina leant into him and did that, her shoe straps dangling from one hand. Gio's belly was hard and flat and she felt his muscles clench as he pushed forward and then back to get them moving. Her arms and hands tightened instinctively around him as the engine roared to life and suddenly they were moving out and into the darkness beyond the racetrack.

The ride was exhilarating through the inky night with the wind whipping past their heads. Valentina gave up worrying about her dress. Her thighs were completely bare by now, clenched tight around Gio's hips.

Her hands were low against his belly and she could feel the tell-tale bulge of his arousal brushing her knuckles. Suddenly emboldened by the decision she'd made, Valentina's fingers opened, exploring, finding Gio's belt, opening it and sneaking her hand underneath to his hot skin.

His hand came over hers and Valentina held her breath thinking he would move it, but he held it there, over his erection, which grew under the palm of her hand, separated only by thin briefs.

It was unbearably sensual, this dark ride into the night, feeling Gio's body respond to her. When at last they turned into his driveway lined with tall trees, Valentina could have wept with relief.

When the bike came to a stop with a throaty roar outside Gio's house, he sat there for a moment, holding her hand on him, before gently taking it off. He turned the engine off and the night was suddenly very still around them. Valentina felt him take a breath and finally unwelded herself from his back, taking her other arm away too.

Gio removed his helmet and then turned around and removed hers. She could feel her hair tumble down around her shoulders. He threw the helmet to the ground and cupped her face in his hands. She could feel the faint calluses against her cheeks.

'What do you do to me, Valentina?'

'The same as you do to me, I think,' she whispered, before Gio slanted his mouth down over hers and kissed her.

When Valentina's hips were rolling impatiently against Gio's buttocks he finally pulled back. They were both breathing hard.

'I think we can do better than kissing on a bike.…' His voice was dry.

Gio got off the bike in one lithe move. He bent down and scooped Valentina up into his arms before she knew what was happening. Her sandals were still dangling from her fingers and they trailed down Gio's back now when her arms went around his neck and she clung on.

Gio shouldered the front door open and Valentina asked dryly, 'No key?'

Gio muttered, 'The security guards knew I was on my way.'

'Oh…' Valentina was stunned again at the sheer evidence of Gio's wealth and reminded herself that he had extremely valuable bloodstock here, some of the most valuable in the world.

He walked them through the dark house. Valentina couldn't make out much in the gloom, just that they seemed to pass through some cavernous empty rooms with big windows before Gio climbed an ornate staircase to the first floor.

He walked them into a room with the door wide open and Valentina could see a huge bed revealed in a shaft of moonlight. Instinctively her arms tightened around Gio's neck. The thought of Gio sleeping in this bed, possibly naked, made her inner muscles clench hard.

Gio stopped by the bed and let Valentina drop to the floor. Her sandals dropped too, from nerveless fingers. His hands were on her bare shoulders and gruffly he said, 'I didn't tell you how beautiful you look.'

Valentina blushed in the gloom and she looked down. Gio tipped her chin back up. 'I'm glad you didn't send them back.'

Her throat felt very constricted but Valentina finally admitted, 'Me too.'

Gio seemed to study her for an infinitesimal moment before he instructed, 'Turn around.'

Silently, tingling all over, Valentina turned around. His hands kept contact with her skin. And then she felt him brush her hair over one shoulder before his fingers trailed from the back of her neck down her spine until they reached the top of the zip.

He pulled the zip down all the way, until she felt his knuckles graze just above her bare buttocks and she shivered. The dress fell open under its own weight and when Gio tugged it gently from her hips it fell to the floor. Gio then undid the clasp of her bra and that, too, was dispensed with.

Turning her back gently to face him, Valentina was glad of the dim light so she couldn't fully make out the expression on his face, in his eyes. She could feel his gaze on her though, making her breasts feel heavy and her nipples spring hard and tight.

When he cupped her breasts in his hands and rubbed his thumbs back and forth over the puckered tips she had to hold on to his biceps to stay standing.

'I want you so much....'

Valentina took a breath and reached her hands up to his jacket, pushing it off his shoulders and down his arms, dislodging his hands from their torturous touch for a moment. Then she made quick work of removing his shirt.

The languor of a few seconds ago was gone. Valentina heard the soft slick of leather as Gio removed his belt and then opened his trousers, pulling them down and off, taking his briefs with them. Desperation mounted. Inexperienced and shaky with the extreme desire rising within her, Valentina all but fell back onto the bed at the merest nudging from Gio. He came down beside her and stretched out so that they touched from thigh to thigh, hip to hip, chest to chest.

Valentina shifted so that she could put her head down on the soft mattress. She reached out a tentative hand to touch Gio's jaw, suddenly suffused with shyness and said, 'Take me...'

CHAPTER NINE

WHEN VALENTINA WOKE she could feel the sunlight caressing her bare skin and a warm breeze, the scent of grass and earth. Superstitiously she didn't open her eyes yet. She was lying face down, on one cheek, and could feel the sheet just covering her bottom. Her legs were splayed with wanton abandon and she had the distinct impression of strong arms that had been around her not so long ago.

She remembered how Gio had tucked her into his body, arms wrapped tight around her, powerful legs cupping her back and bottom as she'd slid into a dreamless sleep with her body humming from the overload of recent pleasure.

She knew Gio wasn't in the room any more. Her skin wasn't tingling with that preternatural awareness. Reluctantly Valentina moved onto her back and winced when aching muscles protested. She blushed when she thought of how tightly she'd gripped Gio's hips with her legs, the way she'd dug her heels into his buttocks, urging him to go harder, *deeper*. She blushed even more when she thought of how she'd dug her nails into his back…he might be marked. And then that thought caused a curiously satisfied glow within her.

Slowly she opened her eyes and took in the room which had been shrouded in darkness last night. It took a few seconds to adjust to the bright light and to realise that there were no curtains on the huge window nearby. Valentina came up on her elbows and looked around.

The room was starkly bare with only a minimum of furniture that looked old and used. A low table with a lamp nearby, a chest of drawers and a wardrobe. The walls were stripped back as if in readiness to be painted. A chandelier light hung over the bed on an exposed wire. Old and unadorned floorboards were unvarnished and uncarpeted.

The feel was very much faded grandeur but not in the artful way that people paid through the nose for; this was the genuine thing. It was as if Gio hadn't cared enough to do it up and something inside Valentina twisted.

Moving slowly, she got out of bed. Huge and equally faded French doors were half open and led out to a private terraced balcony. The view over the surrounding countryside was stunning. In the far distance Valentina could make out what she thought must be Syracuse with the sea behind it, a faint stain of blue.

Conscious of her nakedness, she looked around and saw her dress neatly folded on a chair near the chest of drawers along with her underwear and shoes. She blushed again to think of Gio handling them and then she spotted a T-shirt and a pair of sweatpants laid out over the footboard at the bottom of the bed.

She quickly put them on; they were voluminous but Valentina rolled up the sweats and tied the string tightly around her waist. The T-shirt came to her mid-thighs. After exploring the en suite bathroom which was as undecorated as the bedroom and yet had beautiful antique pieces like a stunning chandelier and a gilt mirror, she went in search of Gio with a distinct prickle of apprehension.

She didn't like to remind herself that they'd avoided this morning-after scenario the other day when she'd confronted him about the tattoo and had a minor meltdown.

Outside the bedroom was a long corridor but Valentina could see stairs in the distance, the stairs that Gio had carried her up last night.

When she went down to the ground floor she could see the huge front door wide open, revealing the courtyard and Gio's motorbike where he'd left it. Flowers trailed haphazardly from pots around the door. Rooms led off the main entrance and Valentina peeked into them. They were slightly more done up than the bedroom but they were still quite bare, with the minimum of furniture.

She came to what had to be the main living room. The walls were white and there was one long low white couch near the middle of the room. A coffee table and a TV seemed incongruous in the huge ascetic room and again Valentina's chest twisted with an emotion she didn't want to look at.

'There you are...'

Valentina whirled around to see Gio leaning against another doorway she hadn't yet noticed, arms crossed. He was wearing a dark T-shirt and faded jeans which hung precariously off those lean hips, the top button open. His jaw was dark with stubble and Valentina recalled how the new growth had felt against her inner thighs only short hours before.

She blurted out, 'I was just looking for you.' She gestured to the clothes awkwardly. 'Thank you...for these.'

He shrugged minutely. 'They look far better on you than they ever did on me.'

Valentina blushed, the enormity hitting her of being here in Gio's house...the morning after the night before.

'Do you want some coffee?'

Seizing any opportunity to block out the revelations coming thick and fast in her head Valentina said quickly,

'Yes, please…and then I really should be getting back to the track.'

Gio lifted a brow as she walked towards him and she stalled.

'It's Sunday, the only thing happening at the track will be the massive clean-up and move-out as people start to transport their horses home. And anyway, it's lunchtime, half the day is already gone.'

Valentina blanched. Lunchtime. Sunday. No escape. Almost desperately now she said, 'My parents…I should see my parents.'

Gio had turned and was walking away, down another long corridor towards the back of the house. He said over his shoulder, 'I rang the clinic earlier and your father is doing fine. They're advising the minimum of fuss before he is taken to Naples tomorrow afternoon.'

Valentina scowled at Gio's back and then immediately felt guilty. He was doing so much for them. Past a constriction in her throat she said, 'Thank you…for checking up on them.'

They were in a huge kitchen now and Gio turned to face Valentina, a small smile playing around his lips as if he knew very well what she'd just been thinking. 'You're welcome.'

Valentina sucked in an involuntary gasp; unlike the rest of the house, the kitchen was pristine. A glorious mix of old and new. Slate floors and rustic wooden worktops blended seamlessly with steel and chrome. Her inner chef sighed with sheer joy. 'This is…stunning,' she breathed out finally, walking towards the central island and running her hand reverently over the surface.

She heard the dry tone in Gio's voice. 'My housekeeper, Eloisa, insisted on the kitchen being finished. It's all to her spec, not mine. She's away this week, visiting family in Messina.'

Valentina thought of the huge cavernous and undecorated rooms. Thankfully Gio's back was to her as he busied himself with the coffee pot. Unable to stop herself, Valentina asked, 'You've lived here for nearly ten years—but it's as if you haven't settled in yet.'

Gio turned around, his face curiously blank, and handed Valentina a tiny cup of espresso. The fact that he knew how she liked her morning coffee made her belly swoop.

Gio took a sip himself and then said, 'In a way I haven't…when I got back from Europe and bought this place it needed a mountain of work.'

Valentina recalled the ongoing construction work whenever she'd been to the *castello* in the past. That's why she'd never been inside before now.

Gio was continuing. 'That took almost two years…and then…'

Valentina's hands clenched so tight around the tiny piece of porcelain that she had to relax for fear of breaking it in two. The significance of what he'd said sank in. Quietly she finished, 'Mario died…'

Gio looked pale and he threw the rest of his coffee back in one gulp before turning to place the cup in the sink.

Valentina put down her own cup and addressed Gio's obviously tense back. 'Where did Mario die?'

He stilled and then he turned around and looked so haunted and bleak for a moment that Valentina quivered inwardly. 'Valentina…' His voice was a hoarse plea.

'Please…I need to know.' To her surprise, she didn't feel angry or resentful. She just desperately needed to know.

As if sensing her intractability Gio moved towards a back door and opened it. Valentina followed to see that it led out to a small herb garden. Obviously the housekeeper's. Gio was holding out a scuffed pair of runners and saying tightly, 'These might fit, they're Eloisa's.'

Valentina took them, avoiding Gio's eyes, and slipped them on. They were a size too big, but fine for now. Valentina had to trot to keep up with Gio as he strode down a path with bushes on either side. Somewhere in the distance she could hear the whinny of a horse.

When they emerged at the bottom of the path the estate was laid out before them. Valentina came to stand beside Gio and saw the vast stables down to their left, surrounded by cypress trees. To the right of that were huge rolling green paddocks, incongruous against the more rocky and bare Siclian landscape and no doubt carefully maintained by Gio's gardeners.

From what she remembered the gallops where Mario had died were behind the stables but she couldn't see them from here. Gio turned to face her, his jaw tight. 'The gallops are gone, Valentina. I got rid of them...after...' His voice trailed off.

She looked up at him. 'What's there now?'

Gio ran a hand through his hair, reluctance oozing from every taut muscle in his body. 'A garden...I got them to cover it over with a garden.'

Determined now, Valentina crossed her arms. 'I want to see it.'

'Why? Valentina—it won't serve any purpose....'

She touched his arm then and felt him tense to her touch which sent a cold shiver down her spine. 'Please, Gio...I need to see this.'

After a long tense moment he took his arm from under her hand and turned and stalked onwards. For the first time since they'd met again Valentina had a glimpse of another side of Gio. Cold, inscrutable. She shivered slightly when she imagined the dynamic between them being very different.

They went down past the stables where lots of curious horses' heads peeped out. Valentina thought she recognised Misfit, who whinnied softly, but she wasn't sure. A couple of stable hands passed them by but they were obviously put off by Gio's expression and scurried on. Valentina only realised then that she was still dressed in Gio's oversize clothes and felt her face flame as she hurried to keep up with him.

He'd stopped before she realised it and she crashed into his back. He put out a hand to steady her but she noticed how quickly he took it away again and felt a dart of hurt. They'd come through an arbour of some sort and were standing in a huge walled garden. Valentina was taking it all in and noticed that Gio was standing on the edge of an elaborate green structure, about a foot high. Valentina came to stand beside him and frowned. 'It's a maze.'

Gio's voice was tight. 'It's a labyrinth. The one path which leads in also leads back out.' She heard him take a breath. 'Mario told me about them once…he'd always been fascinated by them.'

Valentina had a vague memory of Mario mentioning something about them now too.

Gio said from beside her, 'I'll leave you.'

And then he was gone. She could hear him striding away again. It was almost too huge to take in—the fact that there now existed a walled garden where the gallops had been, and then this…labyrinth. Valentina was standing at the entrance and slowly started to walk the path.

It was a curiously meditative experience. Every time she thought she was coming close to the centre of the labyrinth, the path would diverge far away again. She felt exasperated at first until she realised that this was undoubtedly part of the process. She was surprised when she finally found herself stumbling into the centre at last. It was so unexpectedly peaceful that she stood there for long minutes.

She knew her parents would be incredibly emotional to see what Gio had done in Mario's name. And she? Like a coward, Valentina didn't want to explore deeper than the peace she felt right then. Her emotions were far too close to the surface as it was, ambiguous and volatile.

Eventually she wound her way back from the centre to the entrance of the labyrinth and reluctantly left the garden behind. She couldn't shake the feeling that some bruised part of her heart had been healed.

When she got back up to the kitchen door of the *castello* a grim-faced Gio met her. He'd shaved and changed and was holding car keys, and a bag which she suspected contained her dress. 'I can take you now if you're ready to leave?'

Valentina knew that she should be jumping at this opportunity to run as far away as she could, as fast as possible. But in light of Gio's clear desire to have her gone something inexplicably rebellious rose up within her.

She lifted her chin. 'What makes you think I'm ready to leave?'

She saw the quickly hidden flare of confusion in his eyes before they narrowed again. Almost as if wanting to goad her now he said, 'I assumed that seeing where Mario had died would be a passion killer.'

Valentina sucked in a breath at his crude words. But amazingly, hurt didn't grip her. She couldn't articulate it to Gio but it felt *right* to be here with him. Her blood was already flowing thicker in her veins just standing in front of him, his freshly clean scent on the air between them.

'I was the one who wanted to come here, remember?'

Again that flare of confusion. Valentina focused on Gio

and not on the confusing tumult of emotions within her. She walked up to him and took the keys out of his hands and dropped them to the nearby countertop. Then she took the bag out of his other hand and dropped it to the floor.

Gio's eyes were dark, burning. Almost censorious. 'Do you know what you're doing, Valentina?'

Her voice sounded thick to her ears. 'I want you, Gio, that's all.'

Gio smiled and it was grim and hard. 'As long as that's all. I'd hate for there to be any confusion.'

Valentina's heart lurched but she forced herself to say, 'No, there's no confusion.'

Gio reached out and pulled her into his body and Valentina had to fight not to close her eyes at the way her body sang.

'You're right,' he said harshly. 'There's nothing but this.' And then his mouth was on hers and the confusion in Valentina's heart faded away to be replaced by heat.

Just over twenty-four hours later Valentina was standing in a private room in a state-of-the-art clinic in Naples listening to a consultant tell them about the operation which her father would undergo the next day. Her father was in bed, pale, and her mother was sitting by his side, looking worried but stoic, holding his hand tightly.

Gio stood in a corner of the room, arms crossed and face stern as he, too, listened. Dressed in chinos and a white shirt, he looked cool and crisp. And gorgeous, and *remote*.

Valentina's body ached minutely in very secret places. She trembled with awareness just to be this close to Gio. Her brain was still reeling from an overload of sensation and lack of sleep.

She darted Gio a quick glance now but he wasn't looking at her. His jaw was tight, impossibly stern. She felt conflicted, confused. From the moment she'd challenged him in his kitchen yesterday, something unspoken but profound had shifted between them.

She hadn't had time to dwell on it though—Gio had used his considerable skill and experience to render Valentina all but mute with pleasure.

When Valentina had woken late that morning, disorientated and more physically replete than she could have imagined possible, it had been to a cool and fully dressed Gio telling her, 'It's time to go. The plane is ready to take your parents to Naples.'

Valentina's attention came back into the room, guilt washing through her to think that Gio was distracting her even now, when her father's life was being discussed. She did her utmost to ignore him and her roiling emotions and concentrated on her parents.

When the consultant left the room and Valentina had made sure her mother was comfortable in the private room that had been set up for her beside her husband's, all courtesy of Gio, she left, feeling incredibly weary all of a sudden.

She was surprised to see Gio outside the clinic, not sure what she'd been expecting, but half expecting him to have left. Gio faced her now and held out what looked like a plastic hotel room key. 'It's to a suite in the Grand Plaza Hotel. It's not far from here.'

Valentina blanched. It was also one of the most expensive hotels in Italy. She started to protest but Gio took her hand and curled it almost painfully over the card and said curtly, 'I don't want to hear it, Valentina. Take the key and use it. You need to stay somewhere while you're here.'

Valentina reeled at the further evidence of this cool stranger. As if his silence on the journey over here hadn't confirmed that something was very wrong. Suddenly she didn't know where she stood any more; she was on shifting sands. This wasn't the same man who had been clutching her hair, thrusting so deep inside her just hours ago that she'd wept openly.

'I have to go back to Syracuse this evening. But I'll be back to see how the operation went tomorrow.'

Valentina crossed her arms tight against how badly she wanted to touch Gio, have him touch her. To have him explain this abrupt emotional withdrawal. But a deep and endless chasm seemed to exist between them now.

She fought to match his cool distance in a very belated bid to protect herself. 'You don't have to come back tomorrow, you're busy.'

In the same curt tone he replied, 'I'll be here.'

He gestured with a hand to where a driver stood by a car at the bottom of the clinic's steps. 'Dario will take you to the hotel and wherever you need to go. He's at your disposal while you're in Naples.'

'Gio…' Valentina began helplessly before stopping at the look on his face. She threw her hands up. 'Fine, all right.'

Gio stepped back. 'Till tomorrow.'

And then he was gone, down the steps and sliding into the back of his own car before it left the clinic car park and disappeared into the noisy fume-filled Naples traffic, and in that moment Valentina felt as if something very precious had just slipped through her fingers.

Less than an hour later Gio was watching the bright lights of Naples recede from beneath his small private Cessna plane. His gut ached. His whole body ached with a mixture of pleasure and pain. His hands were clenched to fists on his thighs and he had to consciously relax them. He smiled bleakly in recognition of the fact that he could relax them now because Valentina wasn't near enough to him to tempt him to touch her.

Standing on the steps of the clinic he'd had to battle not to pull her into him, bury his face in her hair, feel how those soft curves would fit into his body like missing pieces of a jigsaw.

He'd gorged himself on her for the past twenty-four hours. And it wasn't enough, it would never be enough. But it would have to be enough.

When she'd insisted on seeing where Mario had died, it had spelt the end of the affair to Gio as clearly as if it had been written on a board with indelible ink. When he'd left her standing in that garden, he'd been fully prepared for her return, and for her demand to leave straightaway.

But…she hadn't asked to leave. She'd asked to stay.

And yet it hadn't filled him with a sense of triumph. She'd said, *I want you, Gio, that's all.* And that had reminded him more succinctly than anything else of what was between them. And what *wasn't*. There wasn't even the anger any more.

Valentina had cut herself off from what had happened in the past between them, and she had no problem continuing the physical relationship with him because there was no emotional investment. That's why she hadn't reacted the way he'd anticipated to seeing where Mario had died. That's why she'd had no problem going to the *castello* in the first place.

Gio accepted a tumbler glass of brandy from the attentive air steward. He threw it back in one gulp and winced as the liquid turned to fire down his throat. He cursed himself for having thought for one weak moment that perhaps emotions were involved.

If anything, Valentina's emotions where Gio was concerned had become the worst possible of things: benign.

Soon, Valentina's desire would wane and she would look at Gio with nothing but pity. He'd already seen a flash of it when she'd asked about his house and why it wasn't furnished.

That would be the worst thing of all…to endure Valentina's pity for him. After everything, that was the one thing he wouldn't stand for.

The knowledge sat heavy in his gut. He'd always believed that he was empty inside, after years of contracting inwards to protect himself from his father's cruelty and his mother's ineffectualness. Mario had been the only one he'd trusted and allowed himself to love like a brother. *And Valentina*, a small voice mocked gently.

However, that capacity had died and withered with his friend. He'd believed he'd never love again. But he'd been wrong. The knowledge didn't precipitate joy within him— to discover that he hadn't lost that ability at all. Valentina Ferranti had the power now to tear him apart, there would be no recovery.

'I'm not gone yet….'

'No, Papa, you're not.' Valentina smiled but it felt very precarious as tears burnt the backs of her eyelids. She could feel her mother's steadying hand on her shoulder. The operation had been a big success.

Much to her shame, she couldn't deny that her see-sawing emotions had just as much to do with the huge and silent presence of Gio standing a few feet away in the recovery room, as it had to do with the success of her father's operation.

He hadn't wanted to intrude but her father and mother had insisted on him coming in. Valentina could see her father flagging and immediately a nurse stepped in, saying briskly, 'That's enough for now. You'll have plenty of time to visit again tomorrow. He's going to be here for a while.'

Valentina allowed herself to be hustled out, sharing a quick kiss with her relieved mother, who was staying behind.

Once out in the corridor after Gio had made his goodbyes too, Valentina felt shy and awkward, not knowing how to navigate this new tension between them. It felt like aeons since she'd lain in bed with this man, arms clasped tight around him, her breasts crushed to his chest and her head nestled between his shoulder and neck while his fingers had trailed little fires up and down her spine.

The sense of peace she'd felt in that moment mocked her now.

'I—'

'You—'

They both spoke at the same moment and then stopped. Gio said tightly, 'You first.'

Valentina swallowed. 'I need to get back to Sicily. My mother needs some things from home, now that they're going to be here while my father recuperates.'

'I'm going back now. You can come with me on the plane. I'll arrange for your return when you need to come back.'

So sterile. Valentina shoved down the hurt and forced a smile. 'OK, thanks.' She indicated to the small holdall she held. 'I packed my things and checked out of the hotel just in case....'

Gio was already striding out of the clinic, issuing terse instructions into his phone, and Valentina struggled to catch up to him, a dart of anger piercing her insecurity. What had she been hoping for? She welcomed the anger because it had been a long time since she'd felt it for this man and it gave her the illusion that she still had a shred of control around him.

On the plane Gio made no effort to converse and stared out of his window in silence. The tension grew as the short flight wore on. Eventually Valentina couldn't take it any more and undid her seat belt, turning to face Gio's remote profile.

'Gio…' Her voice sounded unbearably husky.

She could see how his whole body tensed before he turned his head, a brow arched in polite enquiry. Valentina wanted to thump him.

Instead she drew up all her courage. 'Is there something…' She stopped and cursed. He was so damn intimidating like this.

'Is there something wrong? You've…barely said two words to me since…' She gulped and forged on. 'Since we left the *castello* the other morning.'

For a split second Valentina thought she saw something unbearably bleak flash in Gio's eyes but it was gone. She had to have imagined it.

Gio sighed audibly and Valentina felt a shiver of trepidation.

'I don't think we should see each other again.'

'You don't.' Valentina's entire body seemed to go hot and then cold all over. Icy cold.

'Do *you*?' That brow was raised again, like a polite enquiry. As if he wasn't experiencing the same nuclear fallout that seemed to be happening in her body. Valentina had to concentrate on what he'd asked and when she registered how he was looking at her so dispassionately, just waiting for an answer, she blurted out, *'No!'*

She flushed, 'I mean, yes…I think that's a good idea. After all…there's nothing…'

Valentina stopped; she was feeling very light-headed,

breathless. Pain was blooming in her chest and Gio was saying from somewhere distant, 'There is nothing. I think it's for the best. You have your job to get on with. After the Corretti Cup getting work should be the least of your worries. My aunt won't stand in your way again.'

Somehow Valentina thought she managed to get out something that sounded like, 'Yes...thank you...'

The previous couple of weeks flashed through her head, the way Gio had stepped into her life and so comprehensively turned it around. He'd felt obligated; he'd felt the yoke of history heavy around his neck. And he'd desired her. But it was all over now. Finished. Duty and obligation had been seen to and delivered. *There was nothing left.* A small voice mocked her—since when had she wanted anything else? Anything more?

Then the air steward was interrupting them and telling them they'd be landing in a few minutes. Blindly Valentina found her belt buckle and fastened it. The click seemed to reverberate around her head and she looked out the window as the familiar Sicilian landscape rushed up to meet them and kept telling herself, *Breathe, just keep breathing.*

Once the plane had landed and they were on the tarmac Gio turned to Valentina. A muscle ticked in his jaw. 'One of my assistants will take you to get your car at the racetrack. You can let him know when you wish to return to Naples and he'll arrange for your flight.'

Pride stiffened Valentina's spine and to her everlasting relief she felt strong enough to say, 'I can take a scheduled flight, Gio, you don't have to—'

He slashed a hand through the air, making her flinch minutely. And then he cursed softly. 'Just...don't argue, Valentina, please. Take my plane.'

Valentina felt like childishly stamping her foot and demanding why the hell he cared if she went by his plane or not when he clearly never wanted to lay eyes on her again. But just then his phone rang and he lifted it to his ear, not taking his eyes off Valentina, as if daring her to defy him. *'Pronto?'*

As Valentina watched she saw Gio's face turn ashen. He said faintly, 'I'll be right there.'

Impulsively she reached out a hand, scared. 'Gio, what is it?'

He was distracted, looking for his assistant, who came running before turning back to Valentina. 'It's Misfit, he's been taken ill.'

'Oh, Gio…' Her throat constricted and all anger drained away. 'Is there anything I can do?'

Gio stopped for a moment and looked at her, his assistant hovering nearby, and then he just said with chilling finality, 'No, there's nothing you can do. Goodbye, Valentina.'

And then he'd turned and was walking to his low sports car nearby. He swung into the vehicle and with a muted roar was gone. The assistant approached Valentina and took her small case out of numb fingers. 'Ms Ferranti? If you'd like to follow me?'

Two days later Valentina was returning on Gio's private plane to Sicily in the early evening. She'd delivered her mother's clothes and supplies from home. Her father was gaining strength every day and, in all honesty, Valentina knew she hadn't seen him look better in years. What Gio had done, with such effortless ease, had ensured a renewed lease of life to her parents that they could never have attained on their own.

Gio. Valentina felt numb when she thought of him. She still had to clear her things out of the accommodation at the racetrack but felt too weary to think about it straightaway. Her heart clenched when she remembered how ashen Gio had gone on hearing that Misfit was ill. For the first time Valentina realised fully how no one had been there for Gio after Mario died; Mario had been his only, closest friend. A friendship and trust that had been hard won, and which had encompassed her too, once.

When the plane landed Valentina went to her car which was parked in the car park. She sat in it for a long time before making a decision.

When she approached the closed and unfriendly looking gates of Gio's *castello* about thirty minutes later she cursed her impetuosity. A guard approached from an artfully hidden small Portakabin she hadn't noticed before.

'Can I help you?'

She took a deep breath. 'I'd like to see Signor Corretti, please.'

'Is he expecting you?'

Valentina stuttered, her bravado failing her, 'N-no, but if you tell him it's Valentina Ferranti…' *Then he'll tell them that he absolutely doesn't want to see you*, a voice mocked in her head.

Valentina shivered when the security guard disappeared again. She now had an inkling of what it would be like to be on the other side of Gio's affections, and just how much she'd taken his attention for granted.

A long minute later the guard returned and opened the gate saying, 'He's at the stables.'

'Thank you.' Valentina shifted her gears awkwardly as nerves suddenly gripped her. What was she doing here with some misguided notion that she could somehow comfort Gio when he might need it? *You didn't worry about his well-being seven years ago*, her inner conscience mocked her.

Valentina pushed down all the nerves and voices. She

owed Gio at least the courtesy of seeing how Misfit was doing. She knew how much the horse meant to him. She pulled up behind some other cars parked near the stable courtyard and got out.

Dusk was falling but she could see light spilling from the main stables and went towards it. When she entered it took a minute for her to see that Gio had his back to her. He was on his haunches at the entrance to one of the stalls. His back looked impossibly broad as it tapered down to those narrow hips. Hesitantly she went forward and wasn't prepared for when Gio's voice, sounding harsh and husky, said, 'What are you doing here, Valentina?'

CHAPTER TEN

'I...' THE WORDS FROZE in Valentina's throat as Gio stood up and turned around. He looked wild. Unshaven, bleary eyed. His hair was mussed up. He looked as if he hadn't been to bed since she'd last seen him.

She swallowed. 'I was concerned. I wanted to know how Misfit was doing.'

Gio wiped his hands with a towel and threw it down on the ground, then he stepped back and gestured with a hand. 'See for yourself, he's dying. The vet is coming back in an hour to administer the final shot to put him out of his misery.'

Valentina could feel the blood draining from her face. She moved closer to see the huge majestic horse lying on his side with his eyes closed. His whole body was sheened with sweat and his breaths were impossibly shallow.

Eyes huge, she looked at Gio and whispered, 'What happened?'

Gio's voice was sterile, clipped. 'A virus, a very rare virus. It gets into a horse's brain and induces paralysis among other things. The horse sinks into a coma and dies within a couple of days. There's no cure.'

'Gio...I'm so sorry.'

'Why? It's not your fault.'

Valentina winced when she was hurtled back in time

to the graveyard when she'd told Gio it was his fault that Mario had died. Never more than at this moment did she have a full understanding of the pain she'd caused with her grief and anger. Guilt, bitter and acrid, rose upwards.

'Gio...' Her throat ached. 'I'm so sorry...about everything.'

Gio looked at her, his eyes burning in his face. With that uncanny prescience that he seemed to have around her, he knew exactly what she meant. His grim smile did little to raise Valentina's spirits.

'Once...I wanted nothing more than to hear you say that. To know that you possibly didn't despise the very air I breathed.'

The ache in her throat got worse. Valentina shook her head. 'I don't despise...you, the air you breathe.'

'It's too late, Valentina.' He gestured towards his horse. 'Don't you see? It's all too late. Everything turns to dust in the end—it's all completely futile.'

Tears pricked Valentina's eyes now to see the bleak despair on Gio's face. 'No, Gio, it's not all futile, it's *not*. It's terrible that Misfit is dying and I wish he wasn't but he's had a wonderful life with you.'

Gio laughed curtly. 'Just like Mario had a wonderful life until it was snatched out of his hands.'

Valentina reached out a hand but Gio backed away, rigid with tension. He put his hands up as if to ward her off.

Slowly he lowered his hands back down. 'Do you know that I've slowly begun to believe that what happened that night wasn't all my fault? That it *was* just a tragic accident.'

He shook his head. 'We'd finished with the horses and were calling it a night. I still had plenty of time to get Mario home...but then he saw Black Star, loose in the paddock. Mario started to plead again, just for one attempt to ride him, to see if he could possibly have the magic touch....'

Valentina's heart was breaking in two in her chest. 'Gio...'

But he wasn't listening to her, or was ignoring her. 'I wasn't going to let him. I said no and walked to the stables with Misfit. When I got back outside, Mario was putting a saddle on Black Star...I could see the stallion was already edgy. I told Mario to leave it alone...but he wouldn't listen. He'd swung up onto his back before I could stop him, and Black Star went berserk. He jumped the paddock fence but his back leg got caught. Mario went down and Black Star landed on him, crushing him before I could get to him. The damned horse just got up and walked away, dragging Mario behind him until I could get to him and free him... but it was too late.'

Tears were streaming down Valentina's face now, silent sobs making her chest heave. She struggled for control. When she could speak she said thickly, 'You're right, it wasn't your fault...and I should never have—'

Gio put up a hand to stop her speaking. 'No. You had every right to be angry with me. I won't let you take that back now. Nothing can change the fact that it was my fault I had that horse here in the first place when it should have been put down months before....'

Valentina felt exposed and raw. More than anything she wanted to touch Gio...to comfort him. It was like an ache in her whole body. She remembered how cold he'd been when he'd told her it was over. No wonder he never wanted to see her again.

'You won't...' She took in a shuddering breath. 'You won't see me again if you don't want to. I'll stay out of your way.'

Gio just looked at her and Valentina wiped at a tear

on her cheek. And then quietly he said, 'You don't get it, do you?'

'Get what?' She frowned slightly.

Gio took a step closer and something about his intensity made Valentina take a step back. 'See, even now, you show how you really feel.'

'What are you talking about?'

Gio laughed curtly and looked up at the ceiling before looking back down again at Valentina. 'I'm in love with you. I love you so much and it's tearing me to pieces. What was purely physical for you was...*is* soul deep for me. I think I've loved you forever. When you were seventeen I had to pretend to like other girls to stop Mario suspecting that I was only interested in one girl—his sister.'

Gio ran a hand through his hair impatiently. '*Dio*, he would have killed me. *I* would have killed me if I'd been Mario.

'And you?' Gio posed a rhetorical question. 'I know you had a crush on me. I always felt your gaze on me. I noticed the way you'd blush whenever I looked at you.'

Shock was rendering Valentina mute. Her head was spinning. She felt weak and light-headed, like she wanted to sit down on something solid. She couldn't possibly believe Gio had just said he loved her. It was too fantastical, unbelievable.

Gio's mouth firmed; unmistakable pride lit his eyes, turning them green in the soft light. 'I know you don't feel anything for me—I never expected it. Anger and grief fuelled this madness between us.'

Valentina just looked at him, barely hearing his words. She could feel her heart expanding in her chest, as if it had already realised what he'd said and believed it. *Welcomed it*. For a second she saw something like hope in his eyes and her own heart beat faster in response.

She opened her mouth, not even sure what she was going to say, feeling the edges of incredible joy reach out to grab her. The moment hung suspended between them, but then just like that, the spectre of deeply ingrained fear and guilt rose up like a huge shadow to choke her. Memories: the shock of being told Mario was dead, the huge gaping hole left in the family. The excoriating grief and insecurity that had followed. The erosion of belief in anything good, solid, dependable. The awful chasm of loss.

That night in the hospital when for a moment— Valentina shut it down. She couldn't bear for him to see that in her eyes now. The guilt she still felt.

She was standing on the edge of that chasm of loss and pain all over again and she knew she wasn't brave enough to take the leap, to lay herself bare. Her heart spasmed once, painfully. She could feel it contracting in her chest, withering.

She closed her mouth and shook her head minutely in answer to some question that Gio hadn't even asked out loud. The flare of hope died in his eyes, and something died inside her.

Gio turned away from her and picked up the towel from the ground and walked back to the stall. Without turning around he just said, 'The vet is due here soon. Just go, Valentina. We're done.'

Valentina couldn't move though. She was rooted to the spot. She saw Gio's hands come up to the stall posts and grip them so tight that his knuckles shone white. 'Valentina, for the love of God, just…*go*.'

Finally, she could move and Valentina whirled around on the spot before rushing from the stables. Her throat was burning and her eyes were swimming. She almost knocked down the vet, who was just walking away from his car.

When she got into her car it took her an age to start it

up because her hands were shaking so much and when she drove out of Gio's *castello* she had to pull over into a layby where she doubled over with the grief and pain. As she wept and hugged her belly she told herself that this was better, this had to be better than loving and losing all over again, because if she loved and lost Gio…she'd never recover.

Three weeks later…

Valentina looked at herself in the cracked mirror of her tiny bathroom in Palermo. She was pale and wan, dark shadows under her eyes. And her eyes…they looked dead. Valiantly she pinched her cheeks as if that could restore some colour but it faded again just as quickly.

She felt empty and her body was one big ache of loss. She sighed deeply. This wasn't meant to be so painful. The choice she'd made when she'd stood in front of Gio three weeks before… Her mouth twisted at herself. It hadn't been a choice. It had been a deeply ingrained reflex action to protect herself. She was a coward. The worst kind of coward.

Gio. Valentina's hands tightened on the sink—just his name was causing a physical pain in her belly. She'd been terrified she'd see him yesterday when her parents had been brought to a private clinic in Palermo, so that her father could continue his convalescence closer to home.

But it hadn't been Gio who'd come to make sure everything was OK; it had been an assistant, the same assistant who had taken over informing Valentina what was happening. When Gio hadn't shown up, the mixture of relief and pain had been almost crippling.

Her mother had taken one look at her and pulled her aside. 'Valentina—'

And Valentina had cut her off, afraid that the maternal concern would undo her completely. 'Mama, please… don't.'

But her mother had ignored her and said gently, 'Valentina, talk to him. He deserves that much at least.'

Valentina stood up straight. Did Gio deserve that? Did he deserve to hear what she had to say? To hear the awful shameful secret she'd kept secret for so long? The secret her mother knew because she'd witnessed the moment when— Valentina bit her lip so hard that she tasted blood.

For the first time in weeks, Valentina felt a sense of purpose. She would tell Gio…everything. And then if he still wanted her to leave, she would go and perhaps one day this awful yawning ache in her heart would ease.

A couple of hours later Valentina pulled up in the staff car park of the Corretti racetrack. When she got out she asked someone if they knew where Gio was and they directed her to the training ground.

When she got there she could see Gio in the training enclosure. One or two people were gathered around, watching him at work.

The horse pranced skittishly but Gio held the reins firm and murmured low soothing words. Valentina felt weak, her eyes automatically devouring his tall broad form. He looked thinner, leaner. His hair looked messier, as if he hadn't cut it. The lines of his face were unbearably stark and she recalled his bleakness when Misfit had been dying. She recalled the flare of hope dying in his eyes.

She stopped a few feet away from the railing and as if sensing her presence he looked right at her and the air flew out of Valentina's lungs. It was like a punch to the gut and the thought reverberated in her head: *How on earth did I think I could live without this?*

Gio's eyes widened and his mouth opened. And then

everything seemed to happen in slow motion.… As he mouthed her name—*Valentina*—she heard the intense yapping of a dog and saw a flurry of movement to her right as someone burst into the enclosure, clearly chasing the small terrier dog who had no business being in this area.

People started shouting as the dog ran between the horse's feet, barking energetically. Gio's eyes were still on *her* though, with a kind of sick fascination, as the horse reared high and his front hoofs caught Gio on the chest, knocking him backwards. There was a sickening crunch as Gio's head hit off the railing behind him and then he was inert on the ground.

Valentina was unaware of moving; she was only aware of kneeling beside Gio's supine form and holding his head in her lap, his face deathly pale. She took one hand away from the back of his head and it was covered in blood.

She wondered who was screaming hysterically for an ambulance and only realised it was her when someone put a hand on her shoulder and said, 'It's here.'

CHAPTER ELEVEN

'HE'S AS STABLE as can be. He was lucky that his skull wasn't fractured and that his ribs are just badly bruised. He'll be in a lot of pain for a couple of weeks.'

'OK, thank you.'

The doctor looked kindly at Valentina. 'You should go home and get cleaned up. The sedative will have knocked him out for a while.'

Valentina smiled but it felt brittle. 'I'm fine, I'd like to stay.' The doctor eventually shrugged and left the private Palermo hospital room. Valentina had asked them to call Gio's mother but they'd been told that she was away on a short trip. Yet another stark reminder of Gio's isolation which had made her heart bleed.

Valentina turned back to the man lying on the bed. He was covered by a sheet from the waist down, but he was naked from the waist up, with strapping around his chest where his ribs had been injured.

A white bandage was around his head and his face was still almost as white as the bandage. Valentina felt tears burn her eyes again and she went back to the chair beside the bed.

He looked so young and defenceless like this. Sniffling and wiping at the tears that just wouldn't stop, Valentina took Gio's nearest hand in hers. It was completely lifeless.

She bit back the surge of panic and reassured herself that the doctor had said he'd be fine.

A lock of hair had fallen down over the bandage on his forehead and Valentina reached up to push it back. The feel of the silky strands under her fingers made them tremble and she quickly clasped his hand again in both of hers.

Somehow with Gio here like this, not looking at her with that distant expression, it was easier to start talking....

'Gio,' she whispered, 'I know you can't hear me but I need to tell you something—a few things actually. And I know I'm being a coward when you can't hear me....

'The thing is, I don't know if I'm strong enough to tell you when you can look at me and see me for what I really am...and then watch you turn your back on me. I don't think...I could survive that.'

Valentina took in a deep shuddering breath and focused on his mouth. 'The thing is that I love you too. I've loved you for so long, Gio—far longer than I ever admitted it to myself.' Her voice dropped even lower. 'I remember being seventeen and wanting you so much, craving your attention and yet being scared witless of how you made me feel.'

Valentina smiled a watery smile. 'You and Mario together...you were so dynamic, full of life. He never could quite keep up with you but yet he never resented you for it. I think he felt accomplished enough in his own way, separate to you.

'There's something though that I have to tell you—to explain why I've been so angry with you. The evening Mario died...' Valentina stopped for a moment and then went on painfully. 'We got the phone call to say someone was injured, but not *who*. All we knew was that one of you was in trouble and that you were being transported to the hospital in Palermo....'

Valentina felt as if she were standing apart from herself, listening to the story too.

'When we got there, frantic, a doctor came to us and said, "We couldn't save him."' Valentina's hands tightened unconsciously on Gio's.

'The fact was that we still didn't know *who* had died. And I thought…' Valentina's voice broke slightly. 'I assumed that it had been you. The pain was indescribable. But then…I saw you. You were standing there, in the corridor, and the relief was so overwhelming…and then I suddenly realised what that meant. That Mario was dead, not you. And that my worst fear had been losing you, not my own brother.'

Valentina smiled wanly. 'You see, it was only when we saw you that we realised who was dead. My mother had seen my reaction. She *knew* and that merely compounded my own guilt and confusion, along with the pain of realising that it was Mario who was dead.'

She looked down at Gio's hand in hers. 'I've been so ashamed for so long…when I saw you at the funeral I lashed out, unable to bear the fact that you were making me remember that I'd have preferred my own brother to be dead, and he *was*.…

'When I saw you again at the wedding…it all came back. I thought I'd buried it. I thought I'd forgotten you… but I hadn't. And I still wanted you which made things even harder.

'When you told me you loved me, I couldn't believe it. The thought of saying those words back to you…of loving you and possibly losing you the way I'd lost Mario… It was too terrifying…it *is* terrifying. But not as terrifying as it was to see you lying on that ground today.'

Sobs rose upwards again and Valentina choked out, 'The past three weeks have been hell…but I thought that's what

I could live with for the rest of my life. I thought I could protect myself by leaving you…but I can't. I love you, Gio.'

Suddenly overwhelmed with all she'd said, Valentina went to take her hand out of Gio's but to her shock her hand was taken in a tight grip and a soft growl came from the man on the bed, 'Where do you think you're going?'

'Gio…' Valentina breathed out, her heart pumping.

His eyes flickered open slowly and he winced at the bright light for a few seconds before they came to rest on Valentina. Her breath caught in her throat. She was suddenly ridiculously aware of how deranged she must look after hours of crying and the panic-filled helicopter ride to the hospital.

'You have blood on your cheek.…' Gio let her hand go and lifted his to touch her cheek with a finger.

Valentina closed her eyes and prayed for control. 'I… must have got some of your blood on me.…' When his hand dropped again she tried to wipe at it ineffectually with the sleeve of her top.

Nervousness made her babble, and also not wanting to see Gio's reaction as to why she might be there. 'The doctor says you'll make a full recovery. Your ribs are bruised and you've got a nasty crack to the head but it's not fractured.'

Just saying the words though was bringing it all back and Valentina struggled to hold back the tears of emotion.

'I don't give a damn about that.' Gio's eyes were very dark all of a sudden, and alert and intent, on Valentina.

'You don't?'

'No.' He shook his head and then winced minutely when it obviously caused him pain. He opened his eyes again and found and took Valentina's hand in a tight grip. 'What I want to know is did I really just hear you say you love me, and all that other stuff, or was I dreaming?'

Blood was rushing to her head and Valentina whispered, 'How much other stuff did you…think you heard?'

'Everything…I think…' Gio said grimly.

Hesitant, Valentina said, 'About Mario and the hospital?'

'Yes, dammit… Valentina…'

Valentina gripped Gio's hand back and closed her eyes as if that could help. Not to see Gio's face when she said this. 'It wasn't a dream. You heard it, and I meant every word.'

There was silence and after long seconds Valentina opened her eyes again to see Gio with his head back on his pillow and a smile playing around his mouth. 'You love me…'

Feeling slightly disgruntled at his easy insouciance when Valentina felt as if she'd just been pulled from a train wreck she said curtly, 'Yes, I do.'

Gio's smile faded then to be replaced by something more serious. His hand moved up her arm and he said, 'Come here, I need to touch you.'

'But your ribs—your head…I'll hurt you.'

Gio shook his head, this time more gingerly. 'You could never hurt me as much as you did when you walked away after I told you I loved you.'

Fresh tears pricked Valentina's eyes and Gio's hand tightened on her arm. 'But I'll forgive you everything if you just come here right now.'

Carefully Valentina stood up and perched on the side of the bed. Gio's voice was husky. 'Closer.'

Giving in, Valentina kicked off her sneakers and came down full length beside him and tried to ignore his painful intake of breath when he lifted his arm to move it around her so that she was cocooned against him, her head in his shoulder, her hand resting on his abdomen, below the strapping. She felt herself relaxing into his hard form, her curves melting into his body.

She felt him draw a breath into his chest and he said in a carefully neutral voice, 'Why did you decide you wanted to stay at the *castello* after seeing the garden, where Mario died?'

Valentina lifted her head to look at Gio. She remembered the excruciating way he'd shut her out—how ready he'd been for her to flee, because he'd obviously expected her to be upset. She could see now how he might have misread her reaction.

She willed him to believe her, to understand. 'When I saw the garden...and walked the labyrinth, I didn't feel as if Mario was there, or I did...but in a very peaceful way. He always loved visiting you at the *castello* so much. He was so proud of your achievement. I just...I felt happy there, secure. That's why I wanted to stay.'

Gio's arm tightened around her and his eyes looked suspiciously bright for a moment. He sounded gruff. 'I thought...I thought it meant that you'd divorced yourself so much from your emotions around me and what had happened that you just didn't care enough to leave.'

Valentina shook her head. 'Never...my emotions are very much intact.'

Gio touched her chin and jaw with his other hand as reverently as if she were made of china and Valentina felt a profound peace steal over her.

Gio smiled. 'You know what this means, of course?'

'What?'

Gio's eyes glowed dark green with emotion. 'Kiss me first,' he said throatily. Carefully Valentina reached up and pressed her lips to his. Despite the delicacy of Gio's injuries, she could feel his arm tighten around her as the inevitable spark lit between them.

Groaning softly Gio pulled back. Colour was in his cheeks now, replacing that deathly pallor, and Valentina touched his jaw with her hand, her fingers tracing his mouth. Gio kissed her fingers. 'What it means is that you're going to marry me and we're going to live happily ever after....'

Valentina's hand stilled and her eyes widened on his. Giddiness rushed through her entire body but along with it came a tendril of trepidation and she bit her lip. She whispered, 'I'm scared, Gio...I think I'm scared to feel this happy....'

Gio pulled her closer. 'We have love—as long as we have love, there's no need to fear anything.'

'Love..' Valentina smiled tremulously. 'We definitely have love.'

Two years later...

Valentina felt the baby kicking in her belly and automatically put her hand there. She smiled when she sensed a presence and a much larger hand came over hers and an arm snaked around her distended midriff to cup her close to his body. *Gio.* Even now, tremors of awareness went through her especially when she could feel him hardening against her bottom.

One of his hands came up to cup one very full and sensitive breast and her blood got even hotter. Valentina blushed and whirled around within Gio's arms, dislodging his questing hand, and looked up with mock outrage. 'Do you really think your guests have paid to see you mauling your heavily pregnant wife?'

Unnoticed in the background the crowd were going wild as the annual Corretti Cup race was drawing to an exciting finish. Neither Gio or Valentina gave two hoots right then if a unicorn suddenly appeared and won the race instead of the hotly tipped favourite, who was, of course, one of Gio's horses.

Gio smiled lazily, his hand coming back up to cup her breast again, this time kneading it gently so that Valentina couldn't help but moan softly.

'You seemed to enjoy being *mauled* in bed this morning very much if I recall.'

'You're insatiable, Signor Corretti. I'm merely doing my wifely duty to keep you happy.' She smiled prettily and he threw back his head and laughed out loud, infusing Valentina with a bone-deep sense of contentment to hear him sound so happy.

Just then she spotted something out of the corner of her eye and said with happy resignation, 'I think it's time to rescue my parents. Maria's looking suspiciously overexcited and tired which spells trouble.'

Gio turned to follow his wife's gaze and smiled indulgently when he saw his fifteen-month-old daughter squirming to be free of her doting grandparents' embrace. She was trouble, all right, more than taking after her late uncle Mario with her mop of dark brown curls and mischievous eyes.

Gio turned back to Valentina and looked down, his heart swelling with love. Her pregnant belly pressed against him and he felt full up…with love and contentment and peace— for the first time in his life, *peace*.

'We'll rescue them in a minute, but first…'

He didn't even need to say it. Valentina lifted her mouth to his, wound her arms around his neck and they kissed as if for the first time all over again while the crowd went wild behind them, the favourite horse striding easily home to victory.

* * * * *

*Read on for an exclusive interview
with Abby Green!*

BEHIND THE SCENES
OF SICILY'S CORRETTI DYNASTY:

It's such a huge world to create—an entire Sicilian dynasty. Did you discuss parts of it with the other writers?

Yes, we set up a Yahoo loop so that we could discuss our various stories and try to make sure that they all interlinked correctly, and that we had the same details about key events.

How does being part of the continuity differ from when you are writing your own stories?

This is a much more collaborative process than working on your own (obviously!), so it's nice to feel that support from the other authors. Also, we work off a bible that gives us the bones of our stories, so we don't have to worry so much about coming up with the main plot!

What was the biggest challenge? And what did you most enjoy about it?

The biggest challenge is trying to stay within the parameters of the story outline, because the threads in your story have to link in to everyone else's to a lesser or greater degree. What I enjoyed about it most was the fact that I got handed these characters, already fully formed and had to breathe life into them, with my own twist.

As you wrote your hero and heroine, was there anything about them that surprised you?

My hero and heroine were definitely quite different from the types of heroes and heroines I'd normally gravitate to. Valentina had a lot of anger and issues with the hero, and he had to deal with a lot of guilt, mixed with lust! I guess I was surprised at how fiercely Valentina clung on to her anger for Gio, to avoid dealing with her feelings for him, and how patient he was with her.

What was your favorite part of creating the world of Sicily's most famous dynasty?

I loved setting Gio's part of the story in Syracuse, a beautiful part of Sicily. He had set himself apart from the rest of the family and I loved being able to put him somewhere away from where all the main action was happening. It helped to increase his sense of isolation. (Very mean of me :))

If you could have given your heroine one piece of advice before the opening pages of the book, what would it be?

Prepare yourself to meet your conscience!

What was your hero's biggest secret?

Ooh, that would be telling, but it has a BIG part to do with the heroine and his feelings for her.

What does your hero love most about your heroine?

Everything, of course. :) But, what would have initially drawn him to her was her sweet innocence and the way she always looked at him with such artless sensuality.

What does your heroine love most about your hero?

His dark good looks, his sexy charisma. His deep compassion and integrity. His tortured soul, which she can't help wanting to heal.

Which of the Correttis would you most like to meet and why?

I think I'd like to meet Angelo, because he was on the margins of the family, much as Gio always was. An outsider within the Correttis.

#3165 IMPRISONED BY A VOW
Annie West

Billionaire Joss Carmody knows the rules of this game—
he'll shower his new wife with diamonds, and in return
he'll use her land to expand his business. That's all he's
ever wanted, but he hasn't banked on the attraction
Leila awakens.

#3166 A DEAL WITH DI CAPUA
Cathy Williams

Behind Rosie Tom's beauty, Angelo Di Capua knows there
is a deceitful gold digger. But his late wife has left Rosie
a cottage on his country estate—and if she wants to stay,
she'll have to make a deal with the devil!

#3167 DUTY AT WHAT COST?
Michelle Conder

To protect Princess Ava de Veers, bodyguard James Wolfe
must keep his mind on the job. As the passion between
them escalates, they find it harder and harder to resist. But
as royalty, Ava knows that duty *always* comes at a cost....

#3168 THE RINGS THAT BIND
Michelle Smart

Nico Baranski is furious. Does his wife really think he'd just
let her walk away? He'll use every sensual trick he knows
to bring her back. And once he's got her where he wants
her? He'll let her go. But only when *he's* ready!

HPCNM0713RB

REQUEST YOUR FREE BOOKS!

HARLEQUIN *Presents*

2 FREE NOVELS PLUS
2 FREE GIFTS!

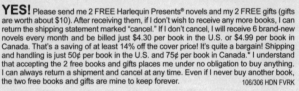

PASSION
GUARANTEED
SEDUCTION

YES! Please send me 2 FREE Harlequin Presents® novels and my 2 FREE gifts (gifts are worth about $10). After receiving them, if I don't wish to receive any more books, I can return the shipping statement marked "cancel." If I don't cancel, I will receive 6 brand-new novels every month and be billed just $4.30 per book in the U.S. or $4.99 per book in Canada. That's a saving of at least 14% off the cover price! It's quite a bargain! Shipping and handling is just 50¢ per book in the U.S. and 75¢ per book in Canada.* I understand that accepting the 2 free books and gifts places me under no obligation to buy anything. I can always return a shipment and cancel at any time. Even if I never buy another book, the two free books and gifts are mine to keep forever.

106/306 HDN FVRK

Name   (PLEASE PRINT)

Address   Apt. #

City   State/Prov.   Zip/Postal Code

Signature (if under 18, a parent or guardian must sign)

Mail to the **Harlequin® Reader Service:**
IN U.S.A.: P.O. Box 1867, Buffalo, NY 14240-1867
IN CANADA: P.O. Box 609, Fort Erie, Ontario L2A 5X3

**Are you a current subscriber to Harlequin Presents books
and want to receive the larger-print edition?
Call 1-800-873-8635 or visit www.ReaderService.com.**

* Terms and prices subject to change without notice. Prices do not include applicable taxes. Sales tax applicable in N.Y. Canadian residents will be charged applicable taxes. Offer not valid in Quebec. This offer is limited to one order per household. Not valid for current subscribers to Harlequin Presents books. All orders subject to credit approval. Credit or debit balances in a customer's account(s) may be offset by any other outstanding balance owed by or to the customer. Please allow 4 to 6 weeks for delivery. Offer available while quantities last.

Your Privacy—The Harlequin® Reader Service is committed to protecting your privacy. Our Privacy Policy is available online at www.ReaderService.com or upon request from the Harlequin Reader Service.

We make a portion of our mailing list available to reputable third parties that offer products we believe may interest you. If you prefer that we not exchange your name with third parties, or if you wish to clarify or modify your communication preferences, please visit us at www.ReaderService.com/consumerschoice or write to us at Harlequin Reader Service Preference Service, P.O. Box 9062, Buffalo, NY 14269. Include your complete name and address.